The Case of the
PERILOUS PALACE

THE WOLLSTONECRAFT DETECTIVE AGENCY

The Case of the Missing Moonstone

The Case of the Girl in Grey

The Case of the Counterfeit Criminals

The Case of the Perilous Palace

THE WOLLSTONECRAFT DETECTIVE AGENCY

№ 4

THE CASE OF THE PERILOUS PALACE

JORDAN STRATFORD

ILLUSTRATED BY KELLY MURPHY

ALFRED A. KNOPF 🐕 NEW YORK

For Zandra

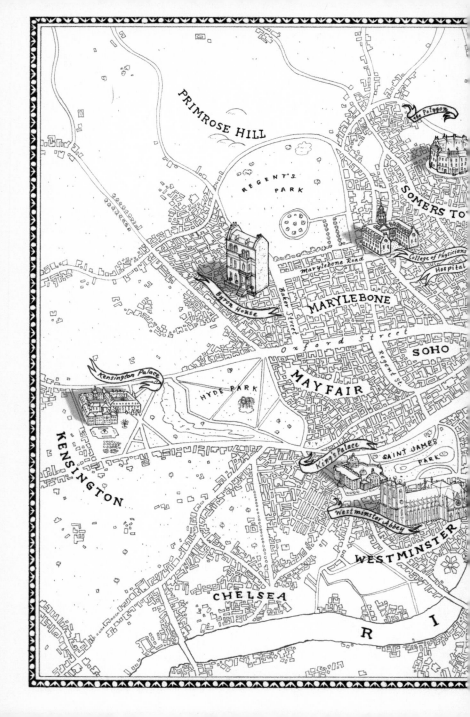

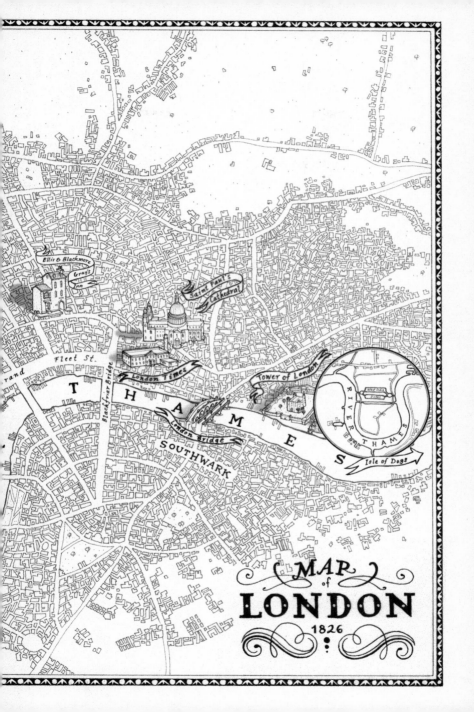

PREFACE

This is a made-up story about two very real girls: Ada Byron, who has been called the world's first computer programmer, and Mary Shelley, the world's first science-fiction author. Ada and Mary didn't really know one another, nor did they have a detective agency together. Mary and Ada were eighteen years apart in age, not three, as they are in the world of Wollstonecraft.

Setting that aside, the characters themselves are as true to history as we are able to tell. At the end of the book, there are notes that reveal more about what happened to each of them in real life, so that you can enjoy the history as much as I hope you'll enjoy the story. Because the history bit is *brilliant.*

—JORDAN STRATFORD

PRECISELY

The click of Ada's door punctuated the end of one sentence and the beginning of another.

The first was a sentence from Gran and came at the end of a long tirade. Ada had missed most of it, noting only that it concerned Ada's having set off a bomb in the house, which was mostly but not entirely true. The bomb had not been a real bomb but merely a counterfeit, smoke-producing bomb, which she had to admit was bomblike enough to be convincing, which was rather the point.

The counterfeit bomb had done its job and

cleared the house of Ada's enemies. Her arch-nemesis, Nora Radel, had mesmerized an alarming number of the household servants, and they had been advancing menacingly when Ada broke the spell and sent them fleeing with a bit of a bang, a lot of smoke, and a cry of "fire!"

The commotion had also sent Gran running from the house, which had seemed like a bonus at the time. But now Gran was back. And she was not impressed with the way Ada had successfully wrapped up her last case. She was not impressed with the Wollstonecraft Detective Agency. Not impressed with Ada's friends, her room, her dress, her anything . . .

The final word of the final sentence of Gran's tirade was "precisely."

"Precisely?" Ada asked, tuning back in, but unclear on what she was meant to be precise about.

"I shall not repeat myself," Gran said with finality, her snotty pug tucked firmly into her armpit.

"You probably should," Ada suggested, only realizing how cheeky that sounded after she'd said it.

And so Gran did. At length. Using words like

"unsuitable," "banished," and "forbidden." And Ada still wasn't sure of much except that all the people she had grown to know or love or care about were being brushed away like crumbs from the arm of a chair. And now even Gran herself was gone, not from the house, but from Ada's avalanche of a bedroom.

With the clicking of the door, a second sentence had begun. This sentence being a kind of imprisonment to which Ada was to be subjected.

Gone—no, banished—was Ada's dearest friend and co-founder of the Wollstonecraft Detective Agency, Mary Godwin, along with Mary's stepsister, Jane. No word was spoken of Ada's half sister, Allegra, because Gran hadn't known she was even there. But if she had known, Allegra would have been banished too. Along with Peebs, her tutor and ally. Anna, Ada's maid, whose name she had only known for a few months, was also dismissed, despite her many years of service.

Ada bundled up the velvet of her gown in little balls in her hot fists and ordered herself not to cry.

The results of this attempt were variable.

"What do we have."

It was not a question, and indeed Ada had no one to ask. The not-a-question was spoken aloud in Ada's disastrous bedroom, which contained sliding piles of books and notes and drawings, tools stained with oil, gears, springs, spindles, and several small jam jars full of dirt, which needed to be sorted. Geographically.

Ada sighed. What the room did not contain was Mary. If Mary were here, Mary could make sense of everything. Or at least ask the sort of questions that would lead to Ada's making sense of everything, which made Mary happy, which made Ada happy. The lack of Mary resulted in a general unhappiness that clung to the damp room like a chill.

The fire had gone out. Of course. Because Anna, tender of fires, was gone.

Ada decided she needed options, and time to think. Her room wasn't perfect for this. It didn't have either her bleh—her mechanical computer—or enough books in it. Taking a look around, Ada admitted that her room probably had the same number of books as the library, but they weren't the right books to solve the problem at hand.

Whatever that was, precisely. She hadn't gotten that far yet.

The library, then.

Ada dared a tiptoe over to her door and turned the knob as silently as she could manage. Peeking out, she spied a footman, stationed just outside her door, preventing any sort of escape—even to the library.

How to get a footman out of the hallway? Ada had very little experience with such things. She knew her way around her butler, the very tall and entirely silent Mr. Franklin. And she'd recently begun to get the hang of maids. The less said about cooks the better, the last one having been under the uncanny influence of a master criminal. It was too much to think about, or at least the wrong time for thinking about it.

She sighed, and returned her attention to her escape.

What little she had observed about her grandmother's footmen was that they were constantly fetching things, and seemed particularly animated after a door-knocking. But how to knock on the door? The windows of Ada's room looked out the back of the house, so it was not as if she could tie a large wrench to a knotted bedsheet and dangle it out the window, in hopes that a good swing could make contact with the front door. No, she'd need to arc the bedsheet straight up and over the roof, hopefully not smashing out any windows in the process.

She found herself sketching a rough diagram of how this might be done, which soothed her. She wondered if her bedsheets, blankets, and bed-curtains tied together would be long enough. Then she remembered that the large wrench she usually kept under her bed had been used to stir up her smoke bomb and sent tumbling down the stairs. So without the weight, the physics was wrong.

A rocket, she thought. A rocket should be able to take a bedsheet up over the snow-covered roof and, its fuel spent, might fall on the other side of the house and knock on the door. But the only way Ada knew how to propel a rocket involved gunpowder, and she'd used all she had on the smoke bomb.

She then realized that a knock on the door would be answered by Mr. Franklin as part of his butlerly duties, and not by the footman outside her bedroom. Ada sighed, and not in a ladylike way, but more like blowing air upward out of her bottom lip, which sometimes made a rude noise by accident.

And that was when she noticed the bell rope.

It had always been there, though she'd never given it much thought. Well, she'd given it enough thought to have, over the years, pulled it for experimental purposes, and swung from it, and tied things to it, and each time it had summoned someone from the depths of the house, usually Anna. She knew that if she pulled it now, a bell would sound belowstairs. The bell was one of many on a board, and each bell was labeled with the name of a room in which a bell rope could be pulled. She remembered seeing the board on her trips down to her basement laboratory. Of course, pulling *her* rope would ring *her* bell, resulting in an unfamiliar maid or footman in *her* room, and that would hardly aid in her escape.

But now an altogether different sketch began to emerge from Ada's pencil. One that mapped a network of bell ropes, cables between walls, and pulleys so that the cables could snake around corners and eventually make their way down to the bell board at the end.

Standing, Ada approached the rope, noticing the point where rope became cable and disappeared into a small hole in a brass plate attached to the wall.

Screwdriver.

Yes, it was as she suspected. Behind the brass plate and inside the not-too-spidery wall was not merely one cable, but several. Ada reached into the wall to feel the taut cords of the bell cables and picked one that wasn't attached to the bell rope in her room. She gave it a tug, and listened.

There it was, a tinkling, down several flights of stairs, faint and distant in the wall's dusty darkness.

After a beat, she could hear doors and footsteps in the creak of the house. Someone was headed somewhere. She tried another cable and pulled, more sharply this time.

Another tinkling, another moment, another set

of summoned steps. It all seemed entirely ordered, which pleased Ada deeply, but what she required in this instance was chaos. She plucked at the cables madly, at random, sending the house's remaining staff room to room, scrambling to find out what was being asked of them.

And finally, there were footsteps right outside her door—the sound of her guard, departing. The bell-rope cables were a system, and Ada had overloaded it. She felt a brief rush of freedom, even though she was still in her room, still in fact up to her elbows in cables, lath, plaster dust, and other wall residue.

Without even bothering to dust herself off, she ran to her door, exhaled, and opened it quietly. While there were many goings-on she could hear, there were no servants to see and, she assumed, none to see her. She stepped into the hallway.

One, two, three steps to the library, and it occurred to her that, while its familiar and comfortable chair and familiar and comfortable books offered more options than her room—options were, after all, the objective of her mission—the basement laboratory promised even more options, including the option of escape from the house, escape, indeed, from her sentence.

She spun about on one stockinged heel and stepped back past her open door toward the door to the servants' stairs. This, she knew well, led to the butler's pantry. From there she could either escape to the back garden or go down farther belowstairs to the kitchen proper, and farther *farther* to the laboratory. Options.

Not hearing any traffic behind the door, Ada opened it, only to discover an imposing grey woman clutching a snarfling and asthmatic pug.

It was Gran, staring directly at Ada. Knowing precisely what she had planned, and merely waiting. In retrospect, Ada felt that the whole thing had been rather obvious, and felt slightly embarrassed by her impromptu scheme.

"Back," stated Gran, pointing.

Ada sighed, again with her bottom lip, hoping it would not emit an accidentally rude noise. In this, at least, she was successful.

THE POLYGON

Mary shook some coals from the scuttle into the fire, the bucket's black weight suddenly gone, so that only hollow tin remained in her hands.

That may have been the last of it, she thought too late, and then worried that the afternoon's warmth would not last through evening. She tucked herself back into her chair by the window.

The Godwins' apartment in Somers Town, a few minutes east of Ada's stately Marylebone townhome, was a cozy jumble of a place, with stacks of books long having outgrown the available bookshelves.

Mary's stepmother, Marie, was hunched over a manuscript at the table, editing pages with a goose quill. Mary's father chuckled at the baby, who was holding tightly to Mr. Godwin's nose.

Mary looked out through the leaded panes of the snow-kissed windows. On her lap was her journal with a story emerging, although she wasn't sure what it was about quite yet. There was also half a map, which had fallen out of a much older book, and while the place names were in an antique typeface, she suspected it might be a part of India. Unless that wobbly bit over there was the Pacific. She wasn't sure, but she was enchanted just the same and wanted to go there wherever it was.

There was something of a clamor in the street. Mary half rose and wiped at the frost to see a long carriage, more for goods than for passengers— trying to ease its way backward through rushing, bundled pedestrians, trying to get closer to her own building.

"Someone is moving in," said Mary. "A family," she added, seeing a clan emerge from various carriage doors, each person burdened with bundles and boxes.

"Chilly day for it," said Mr. Godwin. The baby squeaked happily.

"I do hope they won't be loud," said Mrs. Godwin, not looking up from her papers.

Mary's stepsister, Jane, sidled up to Mary's shoulder for a look.

"I say," Jane said. "Isn't that Charles?"

"Charles is right here," chuckled Mr. Godwin, speaking of the girls' baby brother, who had yet to let go of his father's nose.

"Not that Charles, *our* Charles," stated Jane. It was, in fact, *their* Charles, their friend and accomplice Charles, as Mary could plainly see. Both girls looked at one another and rushed to the door, opening it as they heard Mrs. Godwin's cry of "Capes, gloves, bonnets! You'll catch your death!"

The girls did grab the above and, in a very unladylike display, more or less assembled themselves for the cold as they descended the staircase.

"I wonder if he has a case for us," suggested Jane.

"Doubtful, indeed," said Mary. "I can't imagine

there's much chance of that, what with Ada practically on house arrest, and the lot of us being banished from the Byron house altogether."

"Still, it's a bit curious, don't you think?" asked Jane.

"I find myself eternally curious," Mary laughed.

The door at the bottom of the stairs had a glass front, but it was so frosted over it was impossible to see anything at all. Once open, the door invited December's chill into the hall, which settled with a bite on the noses and cheeks of the Godwin sisters.

Workmen were busy carrying a few worn items of furniture, and they brushed past the girls up the stairs and into their building. There were people who were clearly the parents of *their* Charles, along with an assortment (five, Mary counted) of children who must be brothers and sisters.

At last, their friend made an appearance, with a knowing smile and the doff of his cap.

"Miss Mary, Miss Jane," said Charles.

"Do keep your hat on, Charles. You'll catch your death," said Mary, taking his arm and steering him indoors.

17

"Not today, Mary," said Charles, smiling and following cheerfully.

"Is it true, then?" asked Jane excitedly. "Are you moving in? To the Polygon?" The Polygon being the apt name for their polygonal apartment building.

"Indeed, Miss Jane, and that is a most joyous fact."

"Your new job, is that going well?" asked Mary.

"I begin first thing tomorrow morning. But the promise of my new employment has allowed my family to better their circumstances." Charles had paused just for a heartbeat, and Mary was reminded that much misfortune had befallen the Dickens family (though of course they had never spoken of it). She was gladdened to hear of the improvement in their lot.

"Well, we're delighted to have you as neighbors," said Jane, bobbing past Charles's shoulder to catch glimpses of his family. Mary caught herself looking at her sister in a way not altogether kind, and led the three of them a foot farther out of the doorway to allow workmen to pass by.

"You'll be seeing even less of me, despite that,

I imagine," said Charles. "The solicitors Ellis and Blackmore of Gray's Inn expect much of their clerks. I expect long hours, as I have much to learn."

"You're clever," comforted Mary. "I'm certain you shall have all things sorted in no time."

"'No time,' I'm afraid, Miss Mary, is the matter at hand. As much as I would dearly love to continue to lend assistance in . . . clandestine matters," he said, meaning the Wollstonecraft Detective Agency, "I fear I won't be at liberty—"

"Of course," said Mary. "We understand. And we're delighted for you; I'm sure all of us are. Truth be told, I am not certain there will be any more . . . clandestine undertakings."

"The adventure is up at last, eh?" said Charles.

"For me, at least," said Jane. "It's all been a bit much, to be honest."

"I still hold hope," Mary added, "but with Lady Ada's grandmother in residence, it seems rather unlikely."

"Well, Miss Jane, Miss Mary, I must be getting back to my duties with respect to moving in. Please do send my regards and apologies to Lady Ada."

"I shall, if I can," said Mary. "Though I'm not sure how, and I am sure no apologies are needed. All the same." And she returned Charles's nod as he ducked between the comings and goings of movers and siblings to find himself once more on the steps of the Polygon.

Mary and Jane waited for a similar break in traffic, and headed back upstairs to warm themselves, arm in arm.

So that, thought Mary, was that.

CHOPPING

Ada was rereading yesterday's newspaper. There was nothing, it seemed, she had missed the first time, although she did take note again that the circus was in London for Christmas, a fact her sister might appreciate, if Ada could find a way of letting her know. (Allegra had long harbored a desire to join the circus, and she did have fairly impressive tumbling skills—though Ada would never tell her as much.) There was a picture of circus animals in cages being winched down from ship to dockside. She dropped the grey sheets without folding them, and looked up at the raw and ragged hole she had made in her bedroom wall.

If there are bell-rope cables in the walls, she thought, *why not use the cable-and-pulley system for other things?* Opening doors, or bringing up trays of food, or coal, for that matter. She found herself sketching again.

The shapes she was drawing grew more fantastical and even sprouted wings. This was Ada's latest obsession—wings, flying, and how she might do it. She was reminded of an etching of an ancient animal that swooped about the skies above Devon some thousands of thousands of years ago. A flying dinosaur. A print of the etching was down on a table in her basement laboratory, far out of reach. She could almost see it in her mind's eye.

The design, and of course she thought of it as a design, of the creature's wings seemed perfect. More understandable even than a bird's wing, just skin stretched over thin bones, like bats' wings, like ribbed sails . . .

But no train of thought could stay on its rails for very long when she was cooped up like this against her will. How could her room, her sanctuary, so quickly come to feel like a prison? Ada had seen a prison, and a hospital as bad as a prison, and they were not the same as her current situation, she had to admit.

But in one sense, it was the same. No matter how grand the room, a prison is still a prison.

The bell-rope cables in the wall trembled, shedding a halo of plaster dust. The ceiling creaked. There followed an impossible combination of sounds, footsteps on the roof, a skittering of tools, the creak of ropes . . . and the chopping of axes.

Impossible, she thought. Yet unmistakable.

Ada shot to her door, not caring about the ever-watchful footman. She bolted past him before he could even react, and leapt to the far end of the corridor, to a set of stairs at which she threw herself in a more or less upwardly direction.

At the landing to the attic, two footmen stood stiffly before the firmly closed door. Ada grabbed the sides of their breeches and tried to pry the servants apart, to no avail. The chopping sounds above her were maddeningly louder, and behind her were the precise footsteps of her grandmother, accompanied by the excited wheezing of Charlemagne, the pug, who was happy to be carried upstairs and wondered if there would be some sort of treat at the end, or perhaps someone new to rub snot on.

Ada was unable to stand it. She turned and fired herself like a torpedo down one set of stairs, past Gran and an assortment of servants who dared not reach out to stop her.

Even the foreboding presence of Mr. Franklin at the door did nothing to dissuade her. The very tall butler allowed Ada to escape the house. She shot down the front steps and into the road, where she turned to look up, up, up to the gabled roof of the Byron house in Marylebone.

Two footmen swayed perilously, clinging to ropes with one hand while holding hatchets in the other, chopping away at an entirely different set of ropes: those keeping her precious hot-air balloon secured to the top of the house. With each strike, Ada swore she could smell the jute dust of strong nautical rope whisper like perfume on the wind. Like a goodbye.

Ada's tears were hot on her cold cheeks, her rage fighting with the December chill. She ought to be there, up there on the roof and in the basket of her balloon, repelling the attackers like the pirates they were. She wanted a cannon to fire at them. She wanted a fire poker to thrust at them and parry their axes. She wanted the perfect argument, the most gleaming and glorious logical proof to make them change their minds and cease the ceaseless chopping, chopping, chopping that seemed to hack at her ribs and into her very heart.

She held her breath.

Then the last tendrils of rope failed beneath the hatchets' iron, and the balloon lifted and lurched and lolled gently, ever so gently, away from her house.

Her safety, her refuge. Her balloon. Gone.

And with it her new steam engine, a gift from Peebs. And in the basket were notes, some diagrams of an invention Ada was working on, and also a diary that Ada knew contained the initial fragments of a story Mary was working on. Perhaps even Allegra's snick knife was up in there: Ada had no current inventory of the gondola's contents, and felt a failure beneath the weight of this fact alone.

Every flavor of revenge surged through her blood. A list of those who had wronged her, and most of all, the one who had betrayed her, who had ordered these sliding, reluctant footmen up to the roof with their evil hatchets.

Sister to Viscount Wentworth; wife to Sir Ralph Milbanke, baronet; and mother of Anne Isabella Noel Byron, Ada's mother. It was Ada's own grandmother, the Honorable Lady Judith Noel. Gran. Betrayer.

Ada was astonished to discover how much she could resent and despise a member of her own family.

Ada's brain recited every recipe for every explosion, the physics of every hurling trebuchet or catapult, the distances between the geographies of the farthest ports of call to which a Gran-sized crate might be shipped, Borneo or . . .

All of her rage and revenge was interrupted, not surprisingly, by carriage traffic. Ada actually *was*

surprised, but oughtn't to have been, as she was standing in the middle of the road.

She turned toward the horses, not caring if she was to be trampled. She was a volcano, her blood was lava, and she pitied anyone who dared run her over—not that she pitied them much.

But the carriage stopped. It was the cleanest anything Ada had seen in her life. No common mud dare spatter it; it was a carriage with that degree of importance. A hinged stairway unfolded.

The footman who descended was dressed in velvet livery so heavy that Ada estimated it must equal the weight of a decent dining table. Regardless, the servant carried himself with the elegance of a dancer, and popped off the stair to the street as though the last seven or eight years of his life had involved nothing but rehearsing such a pop. Passing Ada and addressing himself to Mr. Franklin, who stood at the door to her house, the footman announced with a clear, strong bell of a voice: "The Baroness Lehzen, governess to Her Royal Highness the Princess."

And then a woman emerged, of ordinary

appearance despite her grand entrance and the quality of her clothes. She steadied herself with a hand on the carriage (she waved away the assistance of the footman) and looked directly at the distraught, disheveled, tear-stained girl in the street.

"Lady Ada, I presume," said the baroness.

PETULANT

Precisely twenty-four minutes later, Ada, at the upward-shushing hand of her grandmother, rose from the couch as the Baroness Lehzen rose to go.

Gran remained in the doorway, still not sure if she should be pleased, or proud, or horrified.

"Well?" Gran asked once Mr. Franklin had seen out their auspicious guest.

"Well what?" Ada replied.

"You failed to indicate to the baroness that you would of course offer your assistance in her confidential matter, though I must say she does play her cards close, that one."

"She wasn't playing cards," said Ada distantly. She was reviewing her last conversation, unsure if she had all the important bits. Unsure if she had any bits, really. The baroness had turned out to be so well-mannered and polite that she barely seemed to say anything at all. And with Gran haunting the doorframe like that, constantly gesturing for Ada to smooth her gown or improve her posture, Ada was unable to concentrate on what had in fact been said, if anything.

"Surely," Gran tried again, "you could have made your offer of assistance plain."

"No."

"Good heavens, child, what on earth do you mean by 'no' in this instance? It is inconceivable."

"Isn't. I can conceive of it. No. Not helping," came Ada's terse reply.

"Of course you are helping. Whyever would you not?"

"You," said Ada. "Because of you."

"Young Ada, now is not the time to be petulant."

Gran looked at the sulking girl across the room and explained, "'Petulant' means—"

"Insolent. Irritable. Uncooperative. From the Latin *petere,* to attack." Ada's eyebrows were a threat.

"Very well, then," said Gran. "Have you any idea to whom you were just speaking? Why, even your cousin Medora Leigh—"

"Medora?" Ada asked.

"Libby," Gran said with disdain.

"Ah," said Ada.

"Medora Leigh has attended the princess. Many times I've heard." Gran sniffed. "From *that* side of the family. But you, Ada. Did you think how beneficial such a relationship might be to your family, to our standing?"

Ada didn't think her grandmother needed to be standing. In fact, she rather wished the old woman would sit down.

"That," Gran persevered, "was the Baroness Johanna Clara Louise Lehzen, governess to Her Royal Highness the Princess Alexandrina Victoria."

"I have no idea who that is. They is. Are. And even

less of an idea of what they want. But I do know you want me to help, and that means I won't."

"You have no choice in the matter, girl. On that I must insist."

"You insist?" Ada began. "You forbade it just this morning."

"Pish," said Gran, flapping a handkerchief that seemed to have magically appeared for the purposes of flapping.

"'Unsuitable,' you said."

"But this is different," Gran protested. "This is *royalty*."

"You have driven all my friends away . . ."

Gran flapped her handkerchief some more.

". . . and you murdered my balloon, twenty-eight minutes ago."

"That contraption?" Gran's voice rose. "It heralded your demise, child, or worse—scandal. It is my duty to protect you and this family from the latter, at least, if it is within my power to do so. I shall not regret the execution of my duties."

"You shall regret the execution of my balloon," said Ada through gritted teeth. "And don't *pish* me," she added, because she was sure Gran was about to.

"All right," said Gran, crossing the room and finally taking a seat. "What do you want?"

A terrible shadow crossed Ada's face, full of purpose and quiet rage. "I want my balloon back."

"Impossible," answered Gran.

And it was impossible. Even if Ada had an accurate weight of the steam engine and the coal and the balloon itself and the temperature of the air inside it, she still wouldn't know the wind direction or altitude of possible air currents. She had no way of knowing which way her balloon might possibly have blown, except vaguely north. Ish. Yes, Ada acknowledged. Actually impossible.

"Then I want Mary back. And Peebs and Anna and everybody."

"Ada, you are to be in the presence of the princess. Your Mary is hardly of suitable breeding—"

"She is not a horse. She is my friend. And without her I can't help your baroness," said Ada, her frustration growing. "I can't help anybody."

Gran found Ada's frustration contagious. "Oh, honestly—"

"Bell rope." Ada pointed.

Gran was taken aback. "What on earth . . . ?"

"Bell rope," Ada repeated. "Inside the walls of this house is a"—Ada laced her fingers together—"lattice, a network of cables and pulleys. You pull the rope, the cable moves, and it rings a bell on a board belowstairs, in the servants' hall."

Gran blinked, attempting to understand.

"You've cut the bell ropes. I can do the bits in the walls, the tricky bits, that get results. But there's no velvet rope to pull. That's Mary. Nobody else wants to stick their arm in a spooky hole in the wall. I don't mind, but everyone else seems to. No, they want a rope. A nice, soft velvet rope, and Mary is the softest rope in the world."

Gran gave Ada a moment to compose herself.

"Very well," Gran answered. "I shall call for the return of your . . . compatriots. But are you certain about the maid? I can't abide—"

"Anna too," Ada insisted.

"Very well," repeated Gran.

"And you go," said Ada, with an edge of cruelty she herself didn't like.

"Go?"

"You murdered my balloon. I want you to go away. Then I'll speak to your princess."

"She is very much your princess as well, Ada," Gran said softly. "And I shall reluctantly concede. Upon the completion of your assistance to Her Highness, and to Baroness Lehzen, I shall withdraw to Kirkby Mallory." Gran paused. "And your mother may do with you as she will."

Gran rose to leave, and turned with a final word.

"Savor this victory, child, for no doubt its flavor shall turn to bitterness soon enough."

Over Gran's shoulder, a small pug could be seen, cheerfully scooching its bottom along the carpet.

NO MISTAKE

Mary had become used to the company of her sister in the brief carriage rides between the Polygon and Marylebone, so it felt odd to be once more alone on the journey as the coach jerked and bounced and creaked and rattled over the noisy streets of London to some of the smoother and quieter streets of London.

But she had not yet gotten used to the lurching feeling of being welcomed, then denied, then welcomed to Ada's magnificent home across from Regent's Park. There was always a hint of nervousness upon her arrival—would today be a new case, promising adventure? A quiet day of studies in the library? Or another humiliating day of rejection and exile, with someone banishing her from the Byron house forever?

Forever never seemed to last, though, she was beginning to realize. For just that morning one of the new footmen had appeared at the door of Mary's apartment building bearing a note in the hand of Anna, Ada's recently dismissed (and clearly now re-missed) maid, asking her to come to the Byron house at one.

Mary had grown accustomed to the stately home, with its familiar lion's-head knocker, and the tall, ever-silent Mr. Franklin in attendance. But she had never seen the likes of the gleaming carriage that rested outside of Ada's house. Magnificently clad footmen waited expectantly. Even the horses, with their white ostrich-feathered headdresses, were the finest creatures she had ever seen. She wound her way around them, wanting to touch their velvet noses (the horses', not the footmen's) through her gloved fingers, but she dared not. Everything about the carriage seemed pristine and distant. Untouchable, even though it was inches from her hand.

The door opened, and there was Mr. Franklin, as expected. Ada, looking terribly serious as she often did, trotted down the stairs to the carriage as though it were any old coach and not the marvel Mary saw. Ada's expression turned cheerful as she saw Mary, who was moved to hug her friend. She did not, as Ada was not terribly good at being hugged, but Mary held the embrace in her heart just the same.

In the doorway, Anna's capped head popped out behind Mr. Franklin, and she waved a hurried hello before darting in again. Mary smiled. Everything was back in place. Although . . . Mary sensed something was missing, but couldn't think quite what.

Ada was about to step into the magnificent carriage when she turned back to her door.

"Anna!" Ada called. This was met by the return of Anna's head in the doorway. "Glue!"

Anna nodded, and disappeared once more.

"Glue?" Mary asked.

But Ada hadn't heard, or, having addressed the matter, had already put it out of her head.

"Ada," Mary tried again. "How ever did you manage to put things all back together?"

Ada cocked her head in a "follow me" by way of reply, hoisted her dress up a bit to clear the carriage's stairs, and, ignoring the offer of a hand by a footman, disappeared inside. Mary accepted the footman's hand gratefully and climbed aboard.

This is no carriage, Mary thought. *This is a castle.*

The glass seemed more like cut crystal, so the light inside was magnified and magical, sparkling off deep velvet seats, silk cushions, and brocade drapes held back by gold cord. Mary was in awe, though Ada, still lost in thought, seemed unimpressed.

"It is a marvel, is it not?" Mary asked.

"Mmm," answered Ada, who followed up with the not-a-question "What do we have."

"I haven't the foggiest idea, Ada. Anna's note told me to come, and here I am. Let's start with where we're going, shall we?"

"Kensington" was Ada's reply.

"All right," said Mary, patiently awaiting more.

"Palace," Ada added.

"Gosh" was all that Mary was able to muster. She thought she ought to be wearing her best dress, when she remembered she was wearing her only dress.

"Oh!" said Mary, finally understanding what had been odd about the Byron house. "Your balloon!"

"Murdered," said Ada, the heat in her cheeks rising again.

"We are investigating a . . . murder?" asked Mary, with no small trepidation.

"Balloon. Gran. She murdered it."

"I . . . Good heavens. Where did it go?" Mary was alarmed for her friend.

"Gone. North. Ish. East-ish too, I suspect. But gone. Murdered."

"Oh, dear Ada. I am so, so terribly sorry."

"Why are you sorry? You didn't do it."

"It's just what one says, Ada," said Mary.

"Is it?" Ada asked.

"It is," Mary answered.

"Ah." And that was all Mary was likely to get from her companion.

So the pair in their bounceless, squeakless,

rattleless castle glided their way westward toward Kensington. At first.

And then they took an odd left southward, and another winding left, and a winding right, to where the carriage, smooth as it was, began to acknowledge the unevenness of wobbly cobblestones, and the houses faded from white to brick to brown, looming out in their upper stories to peer upon dimmer and poorer streets. It was as though the houses, after standing tall and straight for centuries, had begun to feel the burden of the lives within them, and were sagging with the sadness.

The fine horses with their feathered headdresses stopped on the cobbles. Yet the view beyond the crystalline windows was not that of Kensington Palace but of a shabby and abandoned shop front, shuttered against the lace of snow. *There must be some mistake,* thought Mary.

"No mistake," said Ada.

"Pardon?" asked a confused Mary.

"You were thinking it must be some mistake. It isn't."

"And how ever did you know what I was thinking?" inquired Mary.

"I said 'Kensington Palace,' and this isn't it. So you're thinking either I've got it wrong, or they have. A reasonable assumption."

"However?" Mary asked, leading Ada on.

"However, it's not a mistake, and we are going to the palace. After whatever this place is."

"And what is this place?" Mary thought she ought to feel unsure about the whole thing, but it was hard to feel ill at ease about an adventure that began in a carriage this grand.

"No idea," admitted Ada. "Come on, then." And Ada opened the carriage door a heartbeat before the footman could, hopped out, and marched up the steps to the shuttered shop as though she'd done this a thousand times before. Mary followed as elegantly as she was able, accepting the footman's hand.

A WOMAN OF EFFICIENCY

The door creaked on sleepy hinges, and the little bell attached to it tinkled. It was mercifully warm inside—apparently a fire had been going for several hours.

There were two parts to the store, which was narrow and deep. On the left were thin stairs, and to keep the girls from going up was yet another silent and impeccably groomed footman. On the right, the girls found dusty shelves with cobwebbed curiosities, bits and bobs all with the look of having been thrown away at some point, only to be rescued, placed here carefully upon the rough boards, and then neglected again. At some more recent juncture, the decision must have been made to pass the curio house off as some sort of tea shop, for half a dozen rickety round tables and some questionable chairs had more or less been plopped atop the floorboards, and the tables draped in shabby gingham, long since faded into a mushy pink.

And it was at precisely such a table that the Baroness Lehzen sat, awaiting the arrival of her two guests. But to Ada, this seemed an altogether different Baroness Lehzen than the woman who had made vague inquiries in Ada's own parlor, disclosing little and keeping her manners pristine. No, just a glance told her that this was a woman of confidence. A woman of efficiency.

A woman of secrets.

Mary curtsied, her bonnet, cape, and gloves disappearing in the ballet of footmen, and she nodded in thanks as a chair was pulled out for her and dusted off. Ada slid her own chair backward, its feet skittering and screeching on the boards.

"Miss Godwin, I assume," said Baroness Lehzen to Mary.

Mary, still overwhelmed by the peculiarity of the situation, was too excited to do more than nod. She observed the baroness, a woman of perhaps forty with a long, serious nose and a small mouth atop an endearingly blobby chin.

"And thank you, Lady Ada, for your response. As you can see, I have had to take additional measures to ensure our mutual discretion."

"Junk-shop tea shop," said Ada. "Empty for ages. It's got a . . . whatsit . . . mezzanine, upstairs, but your footman's run up and checked there's no one listening." She nodded, adding a "Clandestine."

"Indeed," said the baroness. "In this environment, we are safe from prying eyes and untrustworthy ears."

"And the palace isn't," surmised Ada.

"Ada—" Mary gasped. Familiar as she was with her friend's practical approach, asserting that the palace was untrustworthy, as though it were riddled with spies, seemed just a step too far.

"No, no, Miss Godwin," interrupted the baroness, "Lady Ada is entirely right. You see, the primary role of myself and ... others is to ensure a safe and appropriate environment for the princess. Her Highness has been an heir presumptive since the sad passing of her father, the Duke of Kent, and she is now just second in line to the throne."

The girls nodded silently as tiny snowflakes filled the air outside and dust motes swirled inside the cozy shop.

Baroness Lehzen continued. "Those of us entrusted with Her Highness's care must observe certain protocols—steps, measures, procedures, that sort of thing—to the letter. This means that the princess has no real privacy at any time."

"At any time?" Mary asked, wondering about specific situations in which her own privacy seemed necessary.

"At any time," repeated Baroness Lehzen. "She is accompanied day and night by either myself or her mother, the Princess Victoria, or by Sir John Conroy, her mother's secretary. At night she sleeps with her mother, or I myself am to watch over her. As Princess Victoria is away visiting family at present, this task falls to me."

"Two Princess Victorias," Ada mumbled. "Confusing. Do you label them?"

The baroness chuckled. "Well, I'm not likely to get them confused. We call the young princess Drina, a nickname for Alexandrina. As she is nine, she is unlikely to be mistaken for her mother."

"Drina," repeated Ada.

"You are to address her as 'Your Highness,' unless invited to do otherwise," cautioned the baroness.

"Drina," said Ada again.

Mary could see this was going to be a challenge.

"Very well," acquiesced the baroness, "between the three of us, and ideally between the four of us, Drina she shall be. Now, this system of surveillance—"

"Always watching," inserted Ada for the benefit of Mary, who was grateful.

"Very good, yes. This system of always watching is very much the invention of Sir John. He has great

influence over Her Highness's mother, and wishes to exert the same influence over . . . Drina, when the time comes."

"What time?" asked Ada.

"The time she assumes the throne and becomes Queen of England," the baroness answered delicately.

"She's only nine," Ada said. "Drina."

"Indeed, Lady Ada."

"So he's going to just stare at her until she grows up?"

"I'm afraid that is very much the case, yes. And I am to be part of this staring-at, as you put it."

"Good grief," sighed Ada.

"Every visit, every meal, every outfit of every day must be carefully recorded and logged and filed away. At the end of the day, Sir John reviews each detail, interrogating us with a barrage of questions. Further, Drina's diary is read nightly by her mother, to ensure that even her innermost thoughts are known."

For the umpteenth time today, Ada's cheeks grew hot. She was outraged that anyone should snoop so, and into one's private diary! She half expected soothing words from Mary, but a quick glance across the table showed Mary's angered expression in sympathy. Invading diaries, both girls felt, was a step beyond the beyond.

"That's why we're here," said Ada. "In this awful tea shop. Because anyone who would pry into a little girl's diary would spy on anything. Including you. Including us."

"I'm afraid you have the matter precisely, Lady Ada," agreed the baroness. "You will find Drina an exceptionally clever girl, though she is self-conscious in certain matters."

This made perfect sense to Mary, who assumed that all people are self-conscious in certain matters.

"Which matters?" asked Ada, which Mary tried not to think rude.

"Drina's mother considers the princess to be . . . chubby. She guards her diet carefully."

"Is she?" Ada asked. Ada couldn't see how being considered chubby was a matter in any regard. "Chubby, I mean."

"Well, I certainly could not say," answered the

baroness. "She is most definitely a very healthy girl, regardless of the opinion of Princess Victoria and Sir John. And before you ask"—which Ada was about to—"the other matter is that of Drina's accent."

"She's English," stated Ada. "Why does she have an accent?"

"Because her heritage is German," Baroness Lehzen explained. "And her mother, and all her courtiers, are German by birth. This has informed the young princess's speech to a degree, and she has been told she does not sound like other English girls. Despite her many talents and virtues, this can make Drina shy under certain conditions."

The girls took it all in. The princess trapped in a tower imprisoned by dragons of people who had convinced her there was something wrong with the way she looked and sounded. Dragons who read her private diaries nightly. They resumed fuming.

Baroness Lehzen raised a hand slightly in an effort to calm the silently seething Wollstonecraft detectives. "I know, and I agree. But it is a thing beyond my power to change. Therefore, Drina and I have devised an alternate method of recording her innermost thoughts, which I shall not state, but trust you will discern of your own intelligence. Yes, Lady Ada, something has gone wrong.

"Something," she said firmly, "that requires your unique, and discreet, attention."

WHAT HAVE WE GOT

Once again, the girls found themselves in the magnificent silk chamber that was the royal carriage, on their way to Kensington Palace. They sat in silence for some moments as dilapidated cobbles and worn wooden blocks gave way to fresher, smoother streets.

Mary had the perfume of a new adventure about her, and her hands tingled with excitement.

"Well?" said Mary, unable to contain herself.

"Well what?" Ada asked.

"We're in a carriage."

"Obviously."

"No, I mean, whenever we're in a carriage after we get the case, you say something," Mary reminded Ada.

"What do I say?"

"You say, 'What do we have,' which I suppose ought really to be a question, but it isn't, not the way you say it. And then we go over all the bits and people in the case."

"Do I?" Ada seemed genuinely intrigued.

"Yes, it helps you relax. Or remember. Or concentrate." Mary nodded. "At least, I think so."

"Ah," said Ada.

"You're not going to say it?"

"You just did, so it didn't seem like I had to." Ada searched Mary's face for the right thing to say, and thought she found it. "It can be your turn."

"Oh!" This seemed to delight Mary. Then she furrowed her brow and plumped up her bottom lip in what, Ada supposed, was meant to be a serious expression. "What do we have."

"Is that me? Are you doing me?" Ada pretended to be insulted by this.

"A bit," giggled Mary.

"Well, then, what do we have, actually?"

"Um," said Mary. "The matter, I suppose, is whatever happened to Princess Drina's secret diary, the 'alternate-method' one that Drina and the baroness devised and that this Sir John fellow doesn't know about."

Ada nodded. "And?"

"Baroness Lehzen, we can assume, is on Princess Drina's side."

"And?" Ada prodded.

"Well, there's Drina's mother, the Princess Victoria, and her secretary, Sir John, who sounds a real cockalorum."

"A what?" asked Ada. "Sounds Latin. But it isn't."

"Ada! A word I know and you don't!" exclaimed Mary. "It really is my turn. A cockalorum is an expression for an unimportant man who thinks he's important."

"Oh," said Ada. "Those."

"Certainly, he's made life difficult for poor Drina, what with snooping on her diary."

And then the streets opened to a majestically tended, snow-frosted park, which gave way to what

seemed to both girls a well-ordered village, in brick. Kensington Palace was no single building but a collection of grand houses, all facing inward to form several square courtyards—and a rather forbidding wall outward.

They had arrived.

POPPYCOCK

"Poppycock," said the thin man with the gold braid on his jacket.

He seemed well put together, with rosy cheeks, a high forehead, and curly hair atop. Handsome, in the way of portraits, Mary thought. But she noticed a desperation in his manner, and a coldness in his eyes she thought she had seen before. Not, she noted, the shiftiness of an imposter. No, more the unsettled and unsettling nature of the treasure hunter. She hoped Ada had noticed as well.

But of course this was ridiculous—what treasure

was there for such a man to hunt? Kensington Palace was an unimaginable perfection of taste and beauty. Food of any sort and of the finest quality in infinite amount was simply the pull of a silk bell rope away. All the riches of England could be before him with a pen stroke.

The girls had bobbed and curtsied their way through the palace. Even Ada had remembered to do this, so overwhelmed by the lush majesty of their surroundings, and Mary knew that took some doing. They were mindful, too, to scrape their boots, and with the subtlest of gestures, a footman indicated that an additional boot scrape was required before stepping inside.

Once the girls were inside, the clockwork gears of formality went spinning: there was a process of "informal" announcements, which were the most formal things Mary had ever witnessed and which sent Ada visibly cringing; and then numerous introductions and inquiries as to the health of Ada's mother and grandmother, to which Ada managed to reply without grinding her teeth down to nubs. And just before she completely lost her temper, there they were, deposited in a small drawing room with a small girl (who certainly didn't strike Mary as particularly chubby, or even if she was slightly, that there was any cause for alarm) and the Baroness Lehzen, who acted as though she'd never laid eyes on either Mary or Ada before. A woman of secrets, Mary remembered.

Before sitting, Ada had turned to quietly address the servant in the hall, only to return a second later, much to Mary's relief. She'd been afraid that Ada was going to make a run for it.

Then, before they'd heard a word from the princess, the word "poppycock" came from Sir John Conroy, who seemed to be having some sort of mild, almost boring argument with himself as he entered the room, just behind them. Mary thought this must be some kind of breach of manners, and wished, not for the first time, her sister Jane were there to navigate such chilly and unfamiliar waters.

"Poppycock!" squawked a brilliantly plumaged parrot in the corner. As colorful as it was, Mary hadn't noticed the bird until just that moment, its exotic nature itself overwhelmed by the sheer luxury of its surroundings.

Mary watched Ada stare at the nine-year-old girl, who appeared to have been set at one end of the room like a doll. Clad in blue velvet, the little girl was blond, with popping blue eyes that matched her dress. She stared back at Ada as if the two of them were having some kind of silent conversation, or playing a very intense game of chess.

Indeed, neither girl had said anything at all to the other. Mary had said a how-do-you-do and curtsied to Baroness Lehzen, but Drina—for it was Drina, and she required no introduction—had glanced pointedly to various spots in the room: two large paintings of presumably dead relatives, a tall clock, a bookcase. Mary followed Ada's lead; the girls needed no code word to know that they were being watched.

"Ah," said Sir John. "Visitors. Excessive."

"Excessive?" asked Ada. The word struck her as odd.

"It means 'very good.' "

"It means 'too much,' " corrected Ada.

"You are malformed," continued Sir John. "I'm sure you're merely inedible."

Now it was time for Ada's eyes to bug out of her head, only this time in frustration.

"Do you mean 'misinformed' and 'uneducated'?" Ada began. "Because I'm glad I'm inedible; that means you can't eat me."

"Inedible!" squawked the parrot.

The baroness rose, interrupting. "Sir John, this is Lady Ada Byron and her companion, Miss Mary Godwin. Lady Ada, Miss Godwin, this is Sir John Conroy, secretary to Her Highness the Princess Victoria." This last bit she added with downcast eyes.

"The big Princess Victoria," added Ada, for Mary's benefit, "not the little one."

None of the grown-ups knew what to do with Ada's breach of propriety, so they did nothing.

"It can be quite confusing," said Princess Drina, finally. Ada noticed that the girl had no discernible accent whatsoever.

This was enough, it seemed, for the whole room to continue breathing.

"And I do insist," the little princess continued, "that you call me Drina. As your cousin does."

"Cousin?" asked Ada, forgetting.

"Yes, Lady Ada," said Baroness Lehzen. "Your cousin Medora Leigh is a frequent visitor to these rooms."

"Oh," said Sir John. "You're *that* Byron. How laborious. Well, then." He did not seem particularly impressed.

Ada knew that "laborious" meant boring, though she suspected the word he was looking for was "notorious," which means famous for all the wrong reasons—something people were always saying about her father.

"Medora?" Ada asked, thinking back to her cousin, yet thrown off by Sir John's malapropism. "Oh, you mean Libby." And upon figuring that out, she didn't seem particularly impressed either. Awkward and uncomfortable as it was, the whole thing was giving her a headache.

A glance between Baroness Lehzen and Mary confirmed that things were not going well.

Drina reached toward a little tiered tray for a biscuit, and stopped to look to the baroness, who in turn looked to Sir John.

He raised a single finger.

Baroness Lehzen nodded, and Drina took only one biscuit from the tray. There was an uncomfortable silence as they all watched the baroness take a small notebook from the side table, and write "one biscuit" next to the time. Ada looked at Mary with disturbed astonishment.

"Shall we play cards?" suggested the baroness.

"I adore cards," said Mary, who didn't actually, but thought it might help if she did.

"I don't know any card games," mused Ada, but realized that she did, and had quite enjoyed them. It had simply been a while, and she had forgotten.

"You can see my drawings, if you like," suggested Drina. And this seemed safe enough to satisfy Sir John, who made clucking excuses and removed himself, leaving the door open.

"I'd like that very much," said Mary, hoping that would keep things going, although where to she could not say.

"Yes, Drina, I think showing them your drawing books is an excellent idea," chimed the baroness.

"Drawings," said Ada, nodding, and finally understanding.

Drina shared with the girls her large, beautiful sketchbooks with very skilled drawings, mostly of the same subject: a small, curly spaniel in a variety of outfits.

"That's Dash," Drina said brightly, "my dog. He's with the grooms at the moment, but you can meet him later."

"Rawrf!" barked the parrot, in an awfully good imitation of a spaniel.

Ada paid more attention to the style of the drawings than to the subject. Drina had a talent for detail. It reminded Ada of her own drawings, and she reached automatically for pencils that disappointingly failed to be there.

There were other books, each weighty and marvelous, and all with meticulous drawings of the things in the room: furniture, drapery, cups and saucers, Drina's own shoes. And several very expert renderings of the parrot, labeled LORY, which was evidently the bird's name. Taken together, it was ultimately a picture of just how small the little princess's world really was, and it made Mary sad after a bit.

The baroness cleared her throat. "Perhaps," she suggested, "the girls might wish to see the doll room?"

Nervously, Drina looked again to paintings, clock, and bookcase. The baroness gave a tiny, almost imperceptible nod, though both Ada and Mary saw it. Drina forced a smile.

"Would you like to see my dolls?" she asked.

Ada really had no interest in dolls, and nearly said so, but then she remembered that the princess was the same age as Ada's little sister, Allegra, and tried to be grown-up by letting her have her way. The fact that Drina was a princess didn't mean that much to Ada, except for the fact that all the bobbing and curtsying she was supposed to remember to do left her exhausted and irritated. She had little patience remaining, having learned almost nothing thus far. Still, she agreed.

"Dolls," said Ada. "Of course." And she squeezed out a smile of her own, though her cheeks didn't like it.

The baroness rose to click open the door at the far end of the room. The palace itself, once she was inside, made little sense to Ada, who counted stairs for comfort and tried to piece together which doors led where. There seemed to have been bits added on to the palace that didn't quite line up with the older bits, and even though this was expertly masked, the inconsistency bothered Ada more than she liked to admit, even to herself.

The narrow door, washed in robin's-egg blue and surrounded by gleaming white, swung open to reveal a kind of dressing room, only it had been converted into a gallery of sorts, with highly polished shelves containing hundreds upon hundreds of dolls.

Mary too had long outgrown dolls, though she appreciated how delicate, rare, and exquisite each piece in Drina's collection was.

Beside each doll was a miniature wardrobe, and once opened (by the gentle hand of the baroness), each revealed a collection of magnificent clothes, tailored for the little figure adjacent.

Drina was once more staring intently at Ada, as though she were trying to stab an idea into Ada's brain through her eyeballs. Which she was.

And it worked.

"Ah," said Ada quietly, realizing.

Drina smiled.

"Right," said Ada cheerfully. "Off we go, then."

"Ada?" asked Mary.

"That's it, visit's over" was Ada's answer. "Lovely to meet you! And I'm not just saying that, although I usually am!"

And without waiting for goodbyes or the escort of footmen, Ada trotted off.

Flustered, Mary curtsied and umm'd several times in succession, and then took herself rapidly down carpeted hallways in search of her friend.

"Visit's over!" squawked Lory the parrot. "Off we go, then!"

INTERLUDE

With several more rounds of hurried yet exhausting curtsies, Mary found herself outside the palace, in front of the magnificent carriage. Inside awaited an unusually patient Ada.

Mary took a gloved hand and climbed aboard, the door silently closed behind her by a well-rehearsed footman. Once seated, Mary noticed that the carriage wasn't going anywhere.

"Clever, that one," said Ada, impressed.

"Which, Ada?" asked Mary. "I must confess I have no idea what happened. It felt to me like the most awkward and uncomfortable encounter in history."

Ada thought of another, and was about to bring it up when she decided to let it go.

"The drawings. The baroness engineered the whole thing. Drina. Brilliant, the lot of them. Well, except that Sir Wrongway."

"Please do slow down, Ada. And why are we not going anywhere?" Indeed, the horses had yet to move, awaiting a knock from within the carriage.

"No, staying here. Going back inside in a minute, actually. The drawings," Ada continued. "The detail. She draws everything."

"I did notice that," said Mary. "A bit sad, really. Obviously, she barely leaves her rooms."

"And yet . . . ," said Ada, smirking.

"Oh, you want me to figure this bit out," realized Mary.

"Yes. Go on, you're clever."

"Well, she has drawings of everything, really. Dog, parrot, furniture. Down to plates of biscuits."

"Except for?" Ada prompted.

Mary reached in her mind for an image of the rooms she'd seen, and recalled seeing drawings of most of it in Drina's sketchbooks. Except for . . .

"Dolls!" Mary squeaked with excitement. "No pictures of dolls at all! So there must be a separate book just for dolls."

"Only she didn't show us that. And for a reason," concluded Ada.

"The reason being?" Mary asked, unsure.

"Do come on—it's obvious. Why don't you show someone something? Because you don't want to, or you can't. She wanted to show us everything else, so that's out. So why can't she? Is it because she's not allowed? Or is it because . . ."

"Is it because she doesn't have it to show! So that's it! That's our case. The book with the doll drawings is missing!" Mary was terribly excited. The missing book of doll sketches certainly resided at the heart of the case.

"Yes," said Ada, agreeing. "But now tell me why it matters."

"Well, it's . . . it's . . . Oh. Oh, yes," said Mary.

"We were watched the entire time. She kept looking at parts of the room where she knows the spies hide."

"And her diary is read every night," added Mary.

Ada nodded. "So any clever girl . . ."

"Would develop a code," said Mary. "And hide it somewhere others might see . . ."

"But not notice," finished Ada. "Specifically, Princess Drina has a sketchbook of her dolls, with the sketches forming a code so that she can write down what she thinks and feels, without anyone being the wiser. Even if they found—or took—the secret diary, all they'd see would be a little girl's drawings of her doll collection."

Both girls blew out big puffs of air, which the dustless carriage failed to illustrate in any way.

"Well," said Mary after a brief silence, "now that we know what's missing, how do we find it?"

"Oh, we go back in now," said Ada. "And look for clues."

"Now? But it's the palace. Don't we need an invitation and all that courtesy and whatnot?"

"Of course not," said Ada. "You forgot your gloves."

"So I did!" Mary exclaimed, just noticing. "But I'm not sure how."

"I got them back from the footman when we

arrived," said Ada, "and dropped them behind a chair. They're still up there. We can collect the clues then."

"Good heavens, you did all that? And what clues?"

"Dirt, under the door. They must clean the floor hourly, with all that staff, but they missed the underside of the door. And there's hair by the fireplace. You collect your gloves, wipe one on the mantel, drop the other one by the door, and catch the dirt from the door bottom when you pick it up."

"I must say, that's more up Allegra's street," said Mary doubtfully.

"You can do it. Besides, we're saving Allegra for later."

"Later?"

"When we break in."

"Break in. To Kensington Palace." Mary was dubious.

"We can hardly investigate while we're being spied on. So we'll have to spy on the spies when they're not looking."

"You can't just ask for a sleepover?" asked Mary.

"I'm not Libby. I can't just do that," said Ada. "Even if I did ask, it doesn't work that way."

"Oh," said Mary. "I'm sorry, I didn't realize. You've never mentioned a cousin before."

"Libby." Ada frowned. "Medora. She gets a whole other name when she's . . . My mum would make me go to court, when I was small. I don't . . . It's too much. Libby was always chatty and she . . . I don't know. She belonged and I didn't. Don't."

"I must say," soothed Mary, "you're doing awfully well. With all of this, I mean." She waved her ungloved hand about the carriage, the palace. All of that. Ada wasn't usually comfortable outside her own home. Or around so many people.

"Hmph," hmphed Ada, quickly changing the subject. "Let's question the witnesses."

"What witnesses? I thought we were gathering clues."

"Drina is under constant surveillance. And there must be half of London working in there as servants. There are witnesses. We just have to find them," Ada said.

"Anyway. Gloves."

LORY

10

The footmen tried their very best to pretend that it was not in any way strange or uncommon for the girls to pop in and then back out of the carriage without going anywhere. Mary wasn't quite sure if Ada relied on others' being too polite to mention her odd behavior, or if she truly didn't realize her behavior was odd. In any event, she charged back up the stairs, and doors opened, and servants stood aside while Ada either pretended they weren't there or honestly forgot to notice. Even Mary gave up on the bobbing and nodding and curtsying, and instead focused on not tripping over the carpet.

By the time Mary arrived in Drina's parlor, Ada had already corralled those whom the girls had met: Baroness Lehzen, Sir John, and Drina herself, in a manner that did not strike Mary as particularly clandestine. But Ada was staring right past all of them, and could not see the expressions of shock on the gathered faces.

"I'm so sorry," Mary tried to soothe. "I seem to have dropped my gloves." Then she made a show of looking all around before spotting them behind a chair and retrieving them.

As she did, a small spaniel in a little red jacket with gold braid on the shoulders rushed in. The dog yapped sharply, and Mary popped up again and Ada turned.

"Dog," Ada said.

"That's Dash," Drina said happily. "My spaniel."

"No, not the spaniel," said Ada, from a great distance. "The parrot," she concluded.

"The parrot?" asked the baroness.

"Lory," Drina clarified.

"Yap!" yapped Dash.

"Inedible!" squawked Lory.

"Indebted," said Sir John, agreeing, though Ada knew he meant "indeed" or perhaps "indubitably," or she would have were she listening, which she wasn't.

"How long does he . . . he?" Ada asked.

"He," Drina confirmed, nodding.

"He stay here? In this room, I mean."

"Always," answered Baroness Lehzen calmly.

"So he's a witness," Ada declared.

"Witness?" asked Sir John, finally getting a word right. "To what?"

Mary remembered her clandestine tasks, so while everyone was focused on Ada, she dropped a glove, made an oh-I'm-so-terribly-clumsy face, and bobbed to pick it up again. There was a smear of dirt on it from the bottom of the door.

"Lory," Ada began. "Have you seen anyone in here, snooping about?"

"I say," Sir John did say. "This is all terribly un-equinox."

Mary was certain he meant to say "unorthodox," or "strange." In fact, he meant it to mean more than that, in a stop-what-you-are-doing-at-once sort of way.

"Oozmansvo denenvuk!" squawked Lory. "As-megratoo!"

"Gibberish," said Baroness Lehzen.

"Does he always do that?" Ada asked Drina.

"No," the princess answered. "He usually repeats what he hears."

"German?" Ada pondered. "Is that German?"

"No," said the baroness, before Drina could answer.

Mary caught an accusing glance between Sir John and Drina, and remembered that Drina was meant to feel guilty for "sounding German," although she certainly sounded English to Mary.

"Perhaps it is Turkish," Baroness Lehzen suggested.

"It's not Turkish," murmured Ada, her head busy. "I know a little Turkish, and that's not quite right."

"Perhaps it's Turkish with a parrot accent?" offered Mary, who suddenly wished she hadn't.

"Might it be Polish?" said Sir John. It was the first

intelligible and practical thing the girls had heard him say.

"Well, does anyone here speak Polish, so that we can figure out what the parrot is saying?" Ada looked at a wall of blank faces.

Drina spoke. "One of the maids is Polish."

Sir John sighed. "You've been speaking to the maids? How inapropeller," he said. He glared at Baroness Lehzen, as though it were her fault.

Ada's eye twitched, but the baroness rose and went to the door, whispering to the footman to fetch the maid. The room waited in awkward silence while the parrot stuck his beak in his armpit, and the dog sniffed things happily.

Shortly, a flustered girl in a maid's uniform, barely older than Drina herself, shuffled into the room and performed an unpracticed curtsy.

"Say it again, Lory," instructed Ada.

"It again," squawked the bird.

"No, no. Like last time. Anyone unfamiliar in here, snooping about?"

"Oozmansvo! Denenvuk!" the parrot declared.

"There," said Ada, turning to the young maid. "Is that Polish?"

The maid looked to Baroness Lehzen, who nodded.

"No, miss," apologized the maid. "If it is, it's not Polish I've ever heard, and my parents speak it at home. Can't speak anything else, you see."

"Very good," said the baroness. "Thank you, you are dismissed."

"Ma'am, if I may," said the maid cautiously, "I think it might be Bulgarian."

"Bulgarian!" exclaimed Sir John.

"Bulgarian!" repeated Lory.

"Do you know anyone who understands Bulgarian?" Ada asked, trying desperately not to roll her eyes.

"The kitchen boy, miss, if it pleases you," answered the young maid.

Baroness Lehzen looked exasperated and put up her hands. Sir John's expression was blank. If he was guilty, Mary noted, he certainly didn't look it.

"Very well," said the baroness. "Fetch him."

It was a few moments before the kitchen boy

86

could be made presentable, and he finally arrived in buckled slippers that were clearly too big for him and a footman's jacket with the identical problem. It seemed a small mercy that no one had been able to find him a wig.

"Bulgarian?" Ada asked, without introduction or explanation.

The boy simply nodded. It was already the strangest day of his life, being summoned so.

Ada merely pointed to Lory, who chimed in with an "Asmegratoo!"

"Bulgarian?" Ada repeated.

"Not Bulgarian," said the boy. "Croatian."

"Oh, for heaven's sake," sighed the baroness, forgetting herself in frustration.

"Croatian," said Ada. "Are you sure?"

The kitchen boy nodded. Mary thought she could hear Sir John's eyeballs rolling in his head out of sheer frustration.

"And is there a chance that you know of anyone in the palace who speaks Croatian?" asked Ada.

The boy shook his head, then stopped, frozen in a fog of thought. "Laundress" was all he said.

"The laundress speaks Croatian," said Ada, making sure.

"Laundress!" cheered on the parrot. Even the spaniel was bored by now.

Baroness Lehzen was holding her head in her hands, and Sir John was wondering if he should leave, or figure out what was going on first. Mary took advantage of this confusion to step toward the fireplace, drop a glove, and then lean against the fireplace to pick it up, while snatching a reddish hair from atop the mantel and folding it into her other glove. She dared not look to the others, but gave the tiniest of nods to Ada.

The scene repeated itself, with the laundress arriving, and insisting that the parrot's now-familiar utterances were indeed not Croatian but German.

"But it's not German," said Ada, seemingly to herself.

"Not German," agreed Drina.

"This is impostulant," said Sir John angrily. "I insect that you deporch at once, innumerably. As you can surly see, the princess is business and cannot entertrain you anymore."

Drina rose, petting Dash as she did so.

"I do wish to thank you for that little game," she said, nodding to Ada and Mary, "and the baroness for orchestrating this instruction. I had no idea how many languages were spoken in this house, and am glad you added this to my tutoring session."

"Tutoring," hrrmed Sir John, wondering if he ought to believe it or not.

"Tutoring!" yelled Lory, which seemed to settle the matter. Still, Sir John stared at them until there was nothing for it but to leave.

"Well done, Drina!" whispered Ada on the way past. Mary did her best curtsy of the day, and thought she detected a pleased look on Baroness Lehzen's face, and a knowing wink from Drina.

EAGLE MID RHO

For the second time, the girls found themselves in a magnificent carriage and not going anywhere, though Mary could swear that Ada had given the proper knock on the glass. Her brain was full and heavy, and it was beginning to pull her face down somewhat, particularly her eyebrows. She needed to go home.

Yet the carriage was not moving. Mary wondered if they had done something wrong. Ada sighed, and knocked again.

This time, instead of silence, the knock was

answered by the door being opened, and one of the footmen presenting a small silver tray, on top of which was a sheet of perfect creamy paper, folded and sealed with red wax. Stamped into the wax seal was a single, elegant letter *L*.

Ada accepted it without acknowledging the footman, and Mary didn't know if this was because Ada assumed they preferred it that way, or if she was just too tired to bother. The door closed as crisply as it was opened, and despite the lack of knock this time, the carriage glided forward.

"*L*," said Ada. "You think it's from Lory, the parrot?"

"The *L* is for Lehzen, I expect," said Mary.

Disappointed, Ada held out the letter, twitched her finger in the direction of Mary's evidence-bearing gloves, and an exchange was made.

"Oh no," said Mary, reading.

"What?" asked Ada, sniffing one glove.

"It is from Baroness Lehzen. It did not go well. She says she wishes we had been more clandestine, and that Sir John has forbidden us to return."

"Mmm," said Ada absently. "Would have got

a better note from the parrot. I suppose that's my fault."

"It's hardly your fault you didn't get a note from a parrot."

"No," said Ada. "The forbidden-to-return bit. My fault, I think."

"Wait," said Mary. "There's something else."

And there was. A tiny slice of paper, scarcely longer than a fingernail and not nearly as wide. Mary took it on her fingertip and handed it to Ada.

"Eagle mid rho," read Ada.

"What on earth could that possibly mean?" said Mary, excited.

"Not sure yet. It's from Drina, though, I'm sure of it. Baroness Lehzen must have been told to write that note at once, and she snuck this clue in there, right under Sir John's nose."

"This is all a bit cryptic," lamented Mary. "We're only guessing about the doll diary, really."

"It's a good guess, though. We'll just go with it until a better guess comes along." Ada changed the subject. "This hair," she said, plucking it from Mary's glove and looking at it until she turned cross-eyed. "Red, wiry. Like a beard hair. Only a very long one."

"I don't think we saw any red-bearded gentlemen in the palace," Mary said. "The servants were all clean-shaven. As was Sir John. What about the other glove?"

Ada turned to the streak of dried mud on Mary's other glove, pressing it up to her nose and inhaling deeply, as if she were starving and there were a roast turkey in the kitchen ready for the table. Closing her eyes, Ada experimentally stuck her tongue on the grainy debris.

In her mind's eye, Ada was no longer in the magnificent silk-and-crystal carriage but in her own room—messy, but with purpose. She imagined her precious jars arranged about her on the floor; she no longer needed to see the labels but imagined sunlight coming up in her room just the same, as each specimen would glint in its own fashion.

She held both images in her mind: her room with her dirt map mirroring all of London, and the peculiar grey-green mud and salt from Mary's glove.

East.

Shoreditch? No, farther still. Hackney, perhaps, but there was no trace of agate in the grains. River mud. South, then, but where? She imagined scanning her jars.

Not river mud, she saw at once. But marsh mud.

"Stepney," said Ada suddenly, opening her eyes.

"I thought you'd fallen asleep!" exclaimed Mary. "Or been poisoned after you licked that muck off my glove."

"We are looking," said Ada precisely, "for a red-bearded man who speaks a guttural language that is neither German, Turkish, Hungarian, Bulgarian, nor Croatian, and has very recently been to Stepney."

"I've never been there," said Mary.

"Neither have I. But I have a very promising jar of marsh mud at home, and I'd like to see where it comes from."

Ada opened the door even though the carriage was moving at a steady clip, which Mary considered a tad reckless.

"I say," said Ada, swirls of snow blowing into the now-chilly compartment. "How long to take us to Stepney? We're going to the Isle of Dogs."

The answer was an entire bum-numbing hour.

At first, the coach had stopped at Marylebone, despite Ada's earlier inquiry. But she assured the footmen that the royal coach was meant to take both girls home, and that (insisted Ada) meant Mary's home as well, which she was pretty sure was farther into East London. And so, not wanting to be rude, the coachman and accompanying footmen bundled their scarves and cloaks higher against the snow, tucking hats lower against the wind, and ventured east.

Ada had always assumed the marsh to be greenish-grey and vaguely unpleasant, like the small jar of mud Charles had collected for her many weeks earlier. She also expected it to be busy, as she knew of the opening of several new shipyards, foundries, warehouses, and roads into what was now one of the most bustling docks in all the world.

But today all was quiet, and it was as if the whole island—which was not really an island, more of a swollen thumb stuck into the river—had gone back to bed and been tucked in with a perfect blanket of white snow.

It was also much larger than Ada expected, with no reasonable way to see everything, and too chilly to leave the carriage and explore. On top of that, Mary found herself getting hungry, and tried her best not to complain.

"Are you certain your home is nearby?" asked a footman, who had up to that point been silent. But he had knocked on the crystal window, and asked his question.

"Oh yes," lied Ada earnestly. "Just round this next bit, I'm quite sure."

Mary smiled, though she felt guilty doing so.

"It's not really fair, Ada," said Mary once the footman had gone.

"What?"

"They're outside freezing, and here we are all toasty warm, and we don't even know what we're looking for."

"Hmm," hmm'd Ada. She half rose from her seat and knocked on the glass. The carriage came to a gentle halt, and the footman reappeared, waiting

patiently while snowflakes settled in his wig and
eyebrows.

"We think you ought to come inside, with us,"
said Ada.

"That wouldn't be proper, miss," said the footman uncomfortably.

"Oh, bother 'proper.' You and your friend should come inside at once."

Mary nodded encouragement at this idea, but the footman remained unconvinced.

"We won't tell anyone," Mary assured him. "Honestly."

The footman clicked his heels together as best as he was able, which wasn't very, as his silk shoes were by now quite squishy with snow. He excused himself, and after a fair bit of astonished muttering with the other footman, both returned to the coach door, whapped snow off one another's shoulders, and climbed aboard with a great deal of bowing and apology, leaving only the coachman outside.

Mary felt bad for him.

"It's, um, just around this bendy bit," said Mary, feeling horrible for lying, yet feeling at the same time slightly better for bringing in the frigid footmen, who were rubbing their hands together for warmth. Rather than their pristine and immaculately put-together selves, the footmen seemed more like ordinary boys, their cheeks red and noses snotty from the cold, with the snow now melting from their wigs and leaving big wet drips on their laps.

Clearly, the entire situation was for them both awkward and uncomfortable, so they settled into more or less pretending that they were not there at all, which seemed to Mary to be a prudent tactic.

Mary herself quietly wondered what all this was

in aid of, seeing as she and Ada didn't even set foot out of the carriage. They simply passed ship after ship, warehouse after warehouse, and lot after lot dumped with giant, rusting chains and huge splintered crates, all covered with snow. Distant sounds of hammering and creaking and shouting would now and then make it between the white muffle and the crystal panes. It had been half an hour, and they had looped all the way round the odd thumb of the old marshlands.

"Very well, then," said Ada after a long silence. "Home now."

The two footmen looked at each other, glanced out at the chill, winced, and nodded to one another. Without bothering to tip their hats at the girls (they were, after all, still pretending they weren't there), they knocked on the glass and barely waited until the carriage had come to a stop before swinging themselves out the door and resuming their demeanor as proper, disciplined palace footmen.

The girls could hear the jingling of all the bits between horse and carriage, and they all clopped along together back west, toward Marylebone.

"I must confess, Ada, I have no idea what all of this was supposed to accomplish," said Mary, more tired and frustrated than she let on.

"The *Trident,* out of Jamaica. The *Wallace,* from India. The *Bonnie Marguerite,* from Borneo. The *Solace,* from Boston in America."

"Those are ship names," said Mary, remembering a few of them.

"The *Cockerel,* from Bristol. The *Donovan,* from Ireland. *La Paloma,* from Portugal," Ada continued.

Mary interrupted. "Well done, Ada! That's a lot to remember. But how do you know where they're from?"

"Flags, sometimes," said Ada. "But usually they have their home ports painted on the bum."

"Stern, Ada. Ships do not have bums."

"All the same," said Ada. "Clues aplenty."

"And any one of those ships might have a red-bearded sailor who speaks something that sounds like Hungarian," mused Mary, disappointed.

"Or Croatian," Ada agreed. "But wouldn't all the sailors from Irish ships be from Ireland, for example?"

"No, I don't think so, Ada. Sailors end up on ships from all around the world. I suspect that's why they become sailors in the first place."

"I didn't know that," acknowledged Ada. "Makes sense." She looked out the window to late December's late afternoon. "Late," Ada repeated, only not really, as she hadn't said it aloud the first time. "We'll have to wait till tomorrow night."

"What happens tomorrow night, Ada?"

"We break into the palace."

"Good heavens! How should we ever do that?" Though this was not the first time Mary had heard of this idea, it was the first time she had been horrified at the thought of it. "There are servants everywhere, and we're specifically forbidden to return. And there are guards, Ada. Actual palace guards. Not like Newgate guards or museum guards, but actual guards with swords and halberds and all manner of whatnot."

"Eagle mid rho," said Ada, as though it were some sort of answer.

"I don't know what that means, Ada," said Mary.

"Me either," admitted Ada.

The royal carriage returned to Marylebone.

It was near supper, and both girls were starving; Mary insisted that she proceed home to help her family with dinner, and Ada insisted that Mary stay and eat something before going home. As usual, Ada was much better at insisting.

Mary marveled once more how different the grand house was from her own, yet even in its grandeur, the Byron house had come to be a sort of refuge for her. She knew its house-sounds, though far quieter than those of her apartment in the Polygon. She knew its smells, from the lavender in the linens to the lemon on the banisters. But the dust of books and the smoke of warming fires were exactly the same, and soothed and thawed her here in what had become a second home.

Anna served them in the library, out of sight of Ada's grandmother. Ada was already building what appeared to be furniture out of the room's many volumes. Atop one stack was a small jar of mud, which

Ada had fetched just to make sure it was a match for the sample on Mary's glove. As Anna brought up the tray of hot soup and warm bread, she took the glove away for a brushing.

"Oh, and Lady Ada, Peebs left this for you," she said, handing over a letter.

Ada already had her nose in two books, so without looking up she waved the thing in Mary's direction. Mary dutifully opened and scanned the letter.

"Peebs regrets not being here, he says. He has some family business at Field Place." She put down the letter. "Field Place, where's that?"

"Field Place, Worthing, Sussex, forty-nine miles away," said Ada, again without looking up.

"Forty-nine miles? It will take him ages in this weather."

"Might it be a counterfeit letter?" Ada asked, more out of habit than anything. "We've had counterfeit letters before."

"Yes, you mentioned that previously. No, Ada, I think it's a perfectly boring, ordinary letter."

"Peebs is boring," Ada agreed.

"I don't think so," said Mary, feeling bad for him.

"Not in a bad way," said Ada. "Just not exciting in a criminal-mastermind kind of way."

"True," said Mary, though wondering if Peebs really did have the makings of a criminal mastermind yet chose not to be one. Looking out at the streetlamps painting the snowflakes briefly gold before they settled, she yawned.

"Yes, you must," said Ada.

"Must?"

"You were about to say you must be getting home."

"You're right, I imagine I was," agreed Mary.

"Anyway, I'll see you tomorrow evening. I have plans to make."

"Ah yes, breaking into a royal palace with armed guards about. Any ideas?" Mary asked.

"That," said Ada, still without looking up, "is what the plan-making is for."

Mary nodded, carefully stepping over the snoring pug that had fallen asleep in the doorway.

STIR-UP DAY

Mary returned home, climbing the stairs to her apartment to find no one in the parlor at all. The entire family was in the kitchen, engulfed in much laughter and the scent of raisins and brandy.

"Mary!" said Jane. "You've been gone for ages. We've already had our turn, now you have a go." She gestured to the pot on the counter, lined with a linen bag, inside of which was a delicious concoction of currants, dried apples, and pears; eggs, milk, and flour; butter and suet; and spices like cinnamon, nutmeg, ginger, and cloves. It was the smell of Christmas, and in the pot was a massive wooden spoon that reminded Mary of one of Ada's wrenches.

"No plums?" Mary asked—this was a bit of a family joke.

"No plums in plum pudding, and that's the secret of it," said Mr. Godwin with a wink. "Go on, Mary, have at it! Give it a proper stir now, or your wish won't come true. Clockwise, mind you, with your eyes closed."

Mary grinned at her family as she took the spoon in her hand and shut her eyes tight.

"Stir, stir!" they chanted, and Mary laughed so hard she couldn't remember what her wish should be, and settled on a happy Christmas for everyone, though she dared not say it aloud lest she spoil it.

"Well done, well done, my darling," Mr. Godwin said. "Now, I'll just have a taste of that . . ."

"You won't, you silly man," insisted Mrs. Godwin, her French accent poking through the words. "This will take at least five hours to boil. Not a crumb before Christmas Eve."

"This will be a proper cannonball," Mr. Godwin

declared, and thus satisfied, scooped up the baby and left the kitchen in search of a book.

The next morning, Mary discovered that plans, apparently, had been made.

A hastily scrawled note and enclosed shillings had been delivered to her door. Jane had intercepted the message, and sensing that clandestine work was afoot, concocted a cover story that Mary was invited to spend the night with Ada. This meant that Mary could avoid lying to her parents. Jane's story was not strictly untrue, but Mary still felt guilty for it.

And yet she was, in the snow, on the edge of Kensington Palace Green. The trees were lit from the glow of the moon reflecting on the snow, and the stars were bright and sharp against a velvet sky. It was enchanting. Like a painting.

All was still. Eerily so. Without a wind, and only the gentlest falling of flakes, all sound was swallowed by the trees.

All sound, that is, save a single *psst*.

Mary looked around, blinking the snowflakes from her eyelashes.

"Psst," repeated the wood. "Mary," it whispered, but in a raspy, loud sort of whisper. Briefly she wondered how the trees knew her name, before she remembered that even if they did, it would be extremely unusual for them to be whispering it, however loudly.

"Hello?" asked Mary of Kensington Palace Green.

"Over here."

Despite her better judgment, and probably because the scene was so pleasant, Mary strode toward the voice.

Suddenly her imagination raced. It was, she was sure, some kind of faerie creature, come to lure her to her fate, lulling her to sleep for a hundred years. Or brigands, perhaps, pirates who would stuff her in some sort of sack and she would awaken in the hold of one of those very ships she had seen the day before, bound for the West Indies, a kidnapped captive.

In the end, however, it was neither faeries nor

pirates, just a particularly bendy nine-year-old girl. Ada's little sister, Allegra.

"Sorry for all the *psst*-ing," said Allegra, her normal voice sounding like cannon fire in the quiet wood. "I was trying to be . . . whatsit . . . sneaky. Only, the word you and Ada use."

"Clandestine," supplied Mary, embracing her friend. Some snow from Allegra's cape brushed Mary's cheek, but she didn't mind.

"That's it. Now, help me with this bag." Allegra shouldered one strap of a heavy canvas sack. Mary took the other, and wobbled a bit to catch her balance.

"Good heavens, what's all this?" Mary asked.

"Rigging," answered Allegra. "All my breaking-into-palace tools."

"You have breaking-into-palace tools?"

"I've been saving them for a special occasion. Isn't that fantastic?" Allegra beamed.

Slowly the two made their way amongst the trees. It didn't feel like trespassing, just a sort of magic.

Every so often, Allegra would suddenly crouch and make a *zzt zzt!* noise, urging Mary to shush,

111

and the girls would hear their weight crunch the snow underfoot, impossibly loudly. Then, with their hearts banging about their ears, they would proceed again.

"What have we been doing?" whispered Mary.

"Timing. Guards," said Allegra. "They don't do much but walk funny."

"It's called marching."

"That. Past that window," said Allegra, pointing to one side of the palace. "Every few minutes or so."

"Where is Ada?" Mary asked, surprised she hadn't done so earlier.

Allegra simply shrugged, and made another series of crunching steps. After a moment, they were close enough to the palace wall they could reach out from behind a convenient bush to touch it. And Mary leaned out to do precisely that.

Allegra grabbed Mary's arm and pulled it back into the bush just as two guards stepped crisply around the corner. Clearly, the guards were no longer visible from the front of the palace, as one began scratching his nose, and the two slowed a little, adjusting their uniforms and dusting snow off their lapels.

Mary's eyes were wide in the moonlight, and Allegra smiled at the thrill of it. They waited for the guards to pass, Mary's blood hammering in her ears.

"Where is Ada?" Mary dared to whisper.

"There's a plan," answered Allegra.

"What plan?"

"I don't know," Allegra admitted. "Just that there is one. Help me with the bag."

They dragged the weighty canvas to the base of the brick wall, and unfastened it. From within, Allegra expertly hoisted ropes, tackle, blocks: all the sort of equipment Mary had seen earlier on the ships at the docks of the Isle of Dogs. Coiling the great ropes around her waist and shoulders, with a soft grunt Allegra pushed herself off the ground, fingers and toes finding tiny, frozen holds in the layers of palace brick.

Up and up she went, at first effortless-seeming, but Mary knew the girl well enough to see the strain, the concentration, and even the fear. Regardless,

Allegra pressed on, weighted by her burden of ship's gear, up even beyond the window to the slight over-hang of the roof and the timbers there, which Mary knew had a name, even if she didn't know what it was.

And that's when Allegra really got impressive.

Toes in the tiny lines between bricks, she bent over backward, grabbing the roof beams, and wove the heavy rope in and out and through little holes in the block of wood she'd hoisted all the way up there. Once the rigging was expertly in place, Allegra wrapped one rope around her foot, held the other in her hand, and descended to the ground lightly as the snowflakes fell all around them.

Mary clapped silently with her gloved hands, and Allegra took a bow.

"That was amazing!" Mary whispered, proud of her friend. "You could join a pirate ship, if you don't find a circus."

"Come on," said Allegra, beaming. "You're next." And in a trice she'd made a loop for Mary's foot and showed her how to hang on. Then Allegra pulled downward on the rope in her hands, and Mary soared up a good two yards in a heartbeat.

"How?" asked Mary.

"Block and tackle," said Allegra, pointing upward. "Ada can explain it. It's in the plan. Anyway, it's brilliant. Look." And with another tug, Mary soared her full height and then some, up the brick wall. So the two proceeded, tugging and soaring, so that Mary could stretch out her hand and barely touch her fingertips on the windowsill above. A few tugs more, and she was looking in the window at the princess's sitting room, where they'd been the day before. Remarkable!

While it was exhilarating, it was not entirely comfortable. The higher she got off the ground, the chillier the wind, which got inside her cloak in ways unexpected. The rope began to tighten around her foot and was now biting. As she tried to adjust, the rope slipped—just an inch, but it was enough to get her heart beating in unpleasant ways.

And suddenly she wished for the unpleasantness in her heart to return, for it ceased beating

altogether when Mary spied the return of the two guards. Allegra had her back to them and so didn't see their approach as she secured the two ropes together in some kind of sailor's knot.

"Allegra! Behind you!" Mary cried. But her voice was lost in the wind, and the guards didn't even glance in her direction as they approached the strange sight of a little girl outside the palace walls, knotting a rope.

"Hello there," began one guard. "What's this, then?"

ON GUARD

13

The two palace guards loomed over Allegra.

"Oh, hello. I'm just breaking into the palace," said Allegra.

"Are you, now?" said the other guard. "How old would you be, then? Ten? You don't look much older than ten, I reckon."

"Aye," the first guard confirmed. "Ten, I reckon."

"Nine, actually," said Allegra with a smile.

"Nine." Both guards nodded, until the first added, "Bit young for a life of crime, now, don't you think?"

"Haven't given it much thought," mused Allegra, finishing her ropework. "Is it crime?"

"Well, it would be, if you broke into the palace," said the second guard, after some consideration.

"Good thing you caught me, then," said Allegra. "Before I could commit any crime, that is."

"Aye, before," said the first guard, a bit confused at this point. "Still, can't have you about to be committing crimes either, eh? Leaving you here with all your criminal intent."

"No," agreed Allegra. "Best we should all get out of here before any sort of crime occurs."

"Well, I think we're quite safe from all that," said the first guard. "I mean, that is to say, we are here for the prevention of such activities. So we should stay."

"All right," Allegra piped in cheerfully. "I'll just go, then, and that's the problem solved."

"Aye, all right," said the first guard, uncertain.

"Hang on a minute," interrupted the second guard.

"Why?" asked the other guard. "She didn't do anything criminal."

"Well, that's because we stopped her," said the second guard.

"But that's your job, isn't it?" asked Allegra. "Stopping crimes? Before they begin, I mean."

"But did you begin?" asked the second guard, even more confused now.

"Only just," admitted Allegra. "But now you've stopped me, so that's a job well done for you fine gentlemen."

"No, no, no," said the second guard. "We've done caught you right and proper, we have. It's not just the stopping; it's the catching." He was quite proud of himself for remembering that part.

"Hmm," Allegra agreed, sounding to Mary very much like her sister. "In that case, you should probably clap me in irons or some such."

"You're only nine," said the first guard. "I don't think we have to do all that."

"Oh, go on, then," said Allegra, sticking her arms forward. "Let's have the irons. Did you bring them?"

"We did, miss," acknowledged the guard.

"Well, on with it, man. It's positively freezing out here."

The guards looked at one another, and seemed to nod with great reluctance. The two worked together to place the heavy shackles about Allegra's tiny wrists, and gestured the way forward to the guard-house.

Mary was horrified, but Allegra would not cease grinning. Then suddenly Allegra let out a huge sneeze, and dropped to her knees in the snow.

"Cor, bless you, miss," said the first guard, helping her to her feet. "Let's get you out of here before you catch your death."

And with that, the three of them marched off into the snow, around the bush behind which the girls had been hiding moments before. But just as the three were disappearing, Allegra looked up to Mary with a wink.

Then Mary realized she was alone, in the December night, which no longer seemed like a painting of a fairyland but a cold world of ice and hard brick, of perilous heights and creaking ropes and hands and feet quickly going numb.

She reached out to the other rope, in hopes that she could either raise or lower herself, but the knot Allegra tied seemed to have done something, and the whole contraption was stuck fast.

She reached out to the palace wall and could just touch the window frame. But holding on there meant not holding on to the ropes, and that wasn't good. Her hands, now frozen in their gloves, gripped the coarse ropes so tightly that little scratchy clouds of rope dust formed and fell in her face, irritating her eyes. She could hold herself like this for a little while, she supposed. But how long? A minute. Not a minute, she realized. Seconds.

The ground seemed even harder and farther away now. Colder too, and more cruel, taunting her. Her fingers were on fire from gripping so tightly, even as her arms complained and weakened.

She dreaded the drop. Despite the fire of courage in her chest, her fingers surrendered, and her doom beckoned.

The *whoosh* of wind she experienced, though, was not from her descent. It came from an enormous pair of scalloped wings, like those of a bat. The terrifyingly large eyes of the beast reflected like glass in the moonlight, and Mary felt its leathery grip tight around her waist.

"Hold on!" said the horror, in a cheerful voice

that sounded remarkably like Ada. Mary quickly realized that the demon from the shadows *was* Ada, and the two of them were sailing over Kensington Palace Green in some kind of bat-winged contraption piloted by Ada. Her frightening eyes were merely glass goggles glinting starlight, and she hugged Mary close with thick-fingered gauntlets. Mary clung for dear life.

"Ada!" cried Mary in relief. "What have you done!"

"Hang on, we're aiming for the roof!"

And with that, there was much swooping and swooshing before both bundled girls tumbled across the snowy tiles of the roof of the palace, not caring if they made too much noise. They slipped and scrambled and rattled, but quickly found purchase not far from the rigging Allegra had wrapped around the roof timbers.

"You saved my life, Ada. With this," said a grateful Mary, who stared with awe at the great ribbed wings on which they had just . . . flown?

"I don't think so. Broken leg at the worst. I thought Allegra would have you in the window by now. Sorry I'm late."

"Allegra!" Mary remembered and, hugging the roofline, scrambled to the edge, over which she could see the two guards running in obvious alarm.

"Oi!!" said the first guard. "Where'd you go?"

Two guards scurried around the corner, not bothering to look up.

Allegra popped out briefly from the bush below, showing Mary and Ada the irons now *off* her wrists and a beaming grin, before disappearing with a wink.

"Ah," said Ada as the guards ran off.

"Remarkable," said Mary to herself, and then aloud.

Ada was busily collapsing the flying wings and harness, strapping them to a chimney for security. Mary marveled at the contraption, which made Ada beam with pride.

"Mr. Franklin salvaged some of the parts from my balloon, so I built something new. I've been studying flyology," Ada said.

"I was not aware that was a thing to be studied," admitted Mary.

"It wasn't until I invented it."

"Ada?" Mary asked.

"Mmm?" Ada answered, removing the goggles from her head.

"How are we to get inside?"

"Well, I was hoping to have Allegra for this bit," Ada said, peering over the roof. "I can't reach that rope from here, but I bet you might."

Mary found she was quite reluctant to have anything to do with ropes again so soon, but Ada was right—she could reach the rope.

"All you have to do is grab on with both hands, walk your way down the wall, and get your feet on the window ledge."

"Is that all?" said Mary, trying to sound braver than she felt, but apparently not succeeding very well.

"All right, then, let me go first." And with that, Ada braved the roof's steep drop, grasped the rope with Mary's assistance, and walked down the wall toward the windowsill.

"Do be careful," urged Mary. The fear for herself had subsided, only to be replaced with concern for her friend. All in all, though, she had to admit that the scene was once again beautiful and mysterious, the whole exercise itself daring and adventurous.

"Got it!" hissed Ada, who had been trying the window, which apparently had no lock. Whoever had built this part of the palace did not consider anyone breaking in by way of rope and pulley, or flying bat wings, and Ada could hardly blame them. She stepped carefully around the opening window, steadying herself, and offering up a hand to Mary.

It was far easier than Mary had anticipated, and within seconds, the two Wollstonecraft detectives were safely inside the darkened room, quietly shutting the window against the wind, the snow from their shoes already puddling the carpet.

THE WATCHERS
IN THE WALLS

Mary said nothing. She knew Ada well, well enough to let her alone so that the clues could start to take shape in the gloom of the princess's parlor. Ada had her sense-making face on, and the thing she was trying to make sense of, at the moment, was the bookcase.

Drina had looked purposefully at the bookcase when they visited, but Mary was unable to see if Ada was scanning for a particular title, or . . .

"Greek," Ada said quietly. "Why must it always be Greek?"

Indeed, Mary could make out the spines of books in the snow-reflected moonlight that spilled in from the window, and yes, some of them were in Greek.

There was a series of nearly identical volumes, all with pinkish-beige covers, and with Greek letters on their spines. Some kind of encyclopedia, perhaps, Mary remembered from her previous researches. But in the midst of them stood a misplaced spine, in dark green or blue—it was difficult to make out precisely in the darkness. What was easy to discern was the image of an eagle, stamped in gold foil, upon the odd book's binding.

Ada decisively reached out with a fingertip, and rocked the book back on its shelf with a satisfying *snick*.

The book was false—a lever for a hidden door behind the bookcase, which silently swung toward the girls.

"Eagle . . . mid rho," said Ada. "That was Drina's clue. *Rho* is the Greek letter on these two books on either side, and here's the book with the eagle. She knew this was here and was telling us how to get in."

"But it doesn't go anywhere," noticed Mary. "It's just a cupboard."

It did look like a cupboard, just barely deep enough to step into, but it ended in a dark, grimy wall, not unlike the space behind Ada's bell rope.

"Not a cupboard," said Ada, stepping in. "A corridor. Look."

As Mary stepped inside, she could see that it was in fact a narrow corridor, which to the right ended in a sharp corner, turning left. A secret passage, in between the walls of Kensington Palace. Fearing that they'd be discovered, Mary pulled the bookcase back to its original place against the wall. Of course, then it was completely dark. And she wasn't sure how they would get out of the passageway again. Mary's heart started beating harder.

"Shh!" shh'd Ada.

"What?" asked Mary. Could Ada really hear her heart?

"Shh!" Ada repeated. And there was something to shh about: a sound. A rumble. Voices? Mary was distracted by the undeniable fact that it didn't smell particularly welcoming there in the scratchy, cob-webby, dark corridor.

There was some light up ahead, though it was not apparent at first where it was coming from. The girls crept closer, until they could make out two dots of light, or rather, two holes, into which light escaped. Ada tried to peer through, but she was too short, and waved Mary over to take a look.

The holes in the wall were clearly eyeholes, and as Mary stood on her tiptoes, she could line them up with her own face perfectly.

This, she realized, is how the little princess was spied upon. She suddenly felt enormously guilty for peeping, then slightly less so as she assured herself that because there was no one in the room, it was no worse than breaking into the palace in the first place.

"It's the painting Drina was staring at," Mary told Ada. "We must be behind it."

Ada nodded.

"I'd built a bit of a map in my head," Ada explained in a whisper, "but it didn't make sense until now. The walls didn't quite line up, but now I know

why." She beckoned Mary to come farther down the grim path, while Mary herself was trying to ignore visions of mice and spiders, or whatever else might haunt the secret passages of palaces.

"How old is this place?" Mary asked, knowing Ada knew.

"Kensington Palace, formerly Nottingham House, built 1605, by Sir George Coppin," Ada rattled off.

Plenty of time to gather ghosts, Mary thought. Still, Mary had faced the prospect of ghosts before, even though—

There it was again, a grinding, growling, grunting, guttural sound, with a note of rasping, scraping at the edges of hearing. Ada froze in the faint light from the eyeholes.

"Is it possible," asked Mary slowly, "that we are not entirely alone in here?"

"Well, obviously," said Ada, a little rudely. She caught herself, and softened her voice. "We know that Drina is always being watched. And we know that Sir John is not the only one watching."

"We do?"

"We do. Drina was popping her eyes out of her

head at the painting even when Sir John was in the room. He probably has other people helping him spy on her."

"What do we do should we run into a spy?"

"Hmm," Ada said thoughtfully. "I didn't get to that bit. In the plan, I mean."

"Should we apprehend them?"

"I think they might apprehend us, honestly," said Ada. "Sorry," she added.

Step by step, they left the tiny island of light behind the painting, and ventured farther into the secret corridor. There was some kind of supporting frame, which the girls suspected might herald some doorway, or at least the division of rooms on either side, and again, ahead, they caught another source of pale light, though larger and dimmer than that which the painting's eyeholes had provided.

Ada stood directly in front of a large, silvery rectangle: a mottled window into the room.

"It's a mirror, I think," whispered Ada. "Into the doll room. It's like a magic trick, a mirror you can see through."

Mary could see row upon row of dolls, their little

dresses and jackets immaculately brushed, their hats perfectly set, their painted faces eerie in silvery gloom. The idea that Sir John, or one of his minions, would stand there simply to observe Drina sorting or drawing her dolls made them both queasy. They prepared to shuffle on.

"Wait, oh, Ada, do wait," said Mary, her eyes squinting.

"What is it?" asked Ada as she peered closer to the false mirror.

"Not through there," said Mary, pointing. "Up here. There's writing."

Someone had taken chalk, or—no, it had to be chalk—and had inscribed something on the wooden slats around the false mirror.

"Image held, or?" read Mary.

"Or what?" asked Ada.

"No, that's what it says. 'Image held, or?' and that's it. That's the whole message."

"That's rude," said Ada. "It's making fun of whoever's on the other side of the mirror. You think it's your reflection, just for you. The image is held by the mirror, or at least it's supposed to be. And here it is, fooling you, letting someone else watch you. It's horrid."

"It is horrid," agreed Mary. "And cruel. But I must confess it is a strange way of putting things."

"I think anyone who would go to all this trouble to spy on a little girl keeps *strange* at the ready."

"Perhaps it's a code?" Mary asked.

Ada considered this. "It's an anagram—a letter scramble—for 'remedial hog.' Possibly other things, but I can't think of any right now."

"Not much of a code," admitted Mary.

"No, let's—" Ada froze.

"What is it?" hissed Mary.

What it was was the sound again, like a heavy chair being dragged against a wooden floor, and a voice at the same time. No words either girl could make out, but more like the idea of words. Coming from the darkness.

"Mary," said Ada stiffly.

"I know," said Mary. "Me too."

"Should we?"

"Probably not. But let's, for Drina's sake," answered Mary bravely. "We've come this far."

"It's funny," Ada said, trying to take her mind off the distant growl, which mercifully had faded. "We've pretended to be criminals before, but now we really are."

"Are we?" asked Mary.

"Breaking and entering," said Ada. "Right now.

This." She waved her hand at the passage between the walls. "Crime."

"I daresay," Mary dared say, "that all this thinking should have perhaps come before the doing."

"We're doing because Drina needs help," Ada insisted.

"Perhaps it's not crime, then?" suggested Mary. "Drina left us that clue. Well, left *you* that clue, which you were clever enough to figure out. The book in the bookcase, which leads to this passage. So that's not breaking, as we didn't break anything, and it's only entering because we were invited."

"That does make sense," agreed Ada.

"Well, then, that should take your mind off . . . things," Mary said, meaning the growling in the distant dark. "And if not, there's the other thing."

"What other thing?"

"I'm embarrassed to say, really."

"Go on, then," urged Ada.

"Well, it's just that it has taken rather a great deal of time to get here, and we're, not stuck exactly, but I'm not entirely certain that . . ."

"Good grief, Mary. Out with it."

"I have to pee," said Mary. "And that's the truth of it."

Ada tried to prevent herself from giggling, and was not altogether successful.

"I know. I just need to find a privy."

"I can't imagine they've built one in the walls," said Ada, which was not encouraging. "Still, this place is huge, and we're sure to run into one, even if it is out there . . ."

"And we're in here," Mary concluded. "Well, let's explore."

"Audentes fortuna juvat," said Ada.

"If you say so."

"Fortune favors the bold," translated Ada.

Mary reached out to Ada's hand and gave it a squeeze.

"Now, come on, then," said Ada, "and try not to think about running water."

"Ada!" giggled Mary.

"Or fountains," Ada added cheekily.

The exchange did a good deal to lighten the girls' hearts, though Mary admitted to herself she was beginning to feel rather uncomfortable.

There was another length of dark corridor, and then another curious turn, and then another, possibly allowing for the shape of rooms, or chimneys. Mary was feeling particularly lost.

"Aha!" whispered Ada. "There's a . . . latch, or something. Closest thing we've found to a door."

"Another bookcase, do you think?" Mary asked.

"Not sure. There's these." Ada pointed to a pair of sliding miniature gates at eye level. "I bet that's for another painting." Slowly she slid the sliders sideways.

"Well?" Mary asked after a full minute, and trying not to think about having to pee.

"I can't see from here. Just the ceiling."

Mary was confused for a moment, but she quickly realized that Ada, being a bit shorter than herself, was looking upward through the holes, rather than directly through them. Mary stepped over to have a look. She was very conscious of her eyes being set into the face of some portrait in the hall, and it was altogether unnerving.

It was a hallway, quite brightly lit despite the hour. And directly across from the painting out of whose eyes she was staring was a narrow oak door with a black handle. A familiar sound of rushing water could be heard, and it made Mary do a small, involuntary dance. The door opened, and a maid exited, wiping her hands on her apron after having washed them in a basin. The maid closed the door.

Mary nodded rather aggressively at Ada, who reached for the latch. It made the tiniest click, but sounded like cannon fire to the two girls.

Just then, a footman approached the oak door. He stood in front of it as though at strict attention, tugged the front of his jacket, and looked left and right, but he seemed to show no sign of having heard the click. Seeing no one, he entered the lavatory.

"Oh no," said Mary.

It was an agonizing few minutes, but finally, the footman emerged, smartly replacing his gloves after having washed his hands. Although instead of opportunity, his exit only invited the arrival of the two palace guards Mary had seen arrest (and then lose) Allegra, on what Ada and Mary could only assume was some kind of routine patrol of the nighttime hallway.

No, it was worse. They were waiting their turn for the privy.

It was Mary's great misfortune to have stumbled across the most heavily guarded toilet in England.

"Mary," said Ada. "I think I've found something."

"Not now, Ada, please." She tried very hard to be quiet.

"No, honestly. There's something here on the latch." Ada had a pinch of something in her fingers, and held it up to the eyehole light. Mary thought it was string, at first, with a glint of red.

"I can't, Ada . . . Can't it please wait just until . . ."

"Mary, it all makes sense now." Ada was increasing in volume as well as excitement. "The *Trident,* out of Jamaica. The *Wallace,* from India. The *Bonnie Marguerite,* from Borneo. Borneo! And I meant to tell Allegra that her circus had finally arrived!"

"Now, Ada, is definitely not the time. I've got to get out of here, and I honestly don't care if they arrest me, provided they let me use the privy first."

"It's not a beard, Mary. The red hair. It's fur! Animal fur!"

The thought was disturbing enough to take Mary's mind off her immediate predicament. It was also alarming that Ada was by now speaking at full volume, and Mary was certain this would lead to their discovery.

More alarming still was the dragging sound, the raspy sound, the grunting sound that did not belong to a red-bearded sailor from not-Croatia, not-Hungary, but to some sort of beast—that sound, *that* sound was closer than ever.

Mary set her hand on the latch, and Ada was about to employ her quietest yell when out of the dark lurched a strange face with a wide, toothy grin.

"Gaah!" cried both girls in accidental harmony. Mary's full weight fell on the now-no-longer-secret panel, and Ada's weight fell upon Mary, and the two tumbled out of the wall and into the hall.

"Gaah!" cried a guard, surprised by the unexpected arrival of young girls falling out of the wall.

"Gaah!" cried the second guard as a strange red beast leapt atop the small pile of girls, and bounced off the opposite wall, bouncing again several times as it sped down the lit corridor toward Drina's parlor, and the window through which Ada and Mary had entered.

The next "Gaah!" was Ada's own battle cry as she scrambled to her feet and gave chase to the creature. That such a sound could come from such a small girl set the guards scurrying in the opposite direction, leaving Mary alone to gather her wits, and decide between her friend and the now-vacant privy.

"Bother," she said, resolved, as she made off in the direction of Ada and her quarry. She ran down the hallway, making an effort not to bounce too much.

It was much quicker going outside the secret passageway than inside it, so it took no time at all for Mary to catch up, and enter the door of Drina's parlor, where she found Ada, alone.

FRUIT

There was no sign of the mysterious beast. She tried to recollect it in her mind, but it was impossible. Covered in fur, like a smallish bear, only with long, gangly arms. The face that had frightened her was grey and wrinkled like an old man's, with tiny eyes set deep into their sockets. Had she imagined it?

"Ada?" Mary asked.

"Shh," Ada answered. Ada stood stock-still in the room, her eyes fixed on the fireplace. All was precisely as it had been the day before: the chairs Mary and Ada had sat in, the chairs for the baroness and princess. The tall stand in the corner, complete with parrot, who was at the moment clearly asleep, his head tucked under his wing of orange and emerald.

"Lady Ada?" said Drina, entering the room in her nightdress.

"Shh," Ada answered.

"Lady Ada?" said Baroness Lehzen, entering the room in *her* nightdress.

"Shh," Ada answered. "Honestly, everyone."

There was a clatter and clamor in the doorway, and in strode the two guards from earlier, flanking a disgruntled-looking Sir John, who, mercifully, was not in his nightdress.

"What is all this connotation?" he bellowed.

"Commotion," corrected Ada. "And *shh*. Bring me some fruit."

"Fruit!" screeched Lory the parrot, who had suddenly woken up.

"I beg your paddle?" said Sir John, clearly flustered.

"Pardon. Fruit," said Ada. "Bring. Now."

"I cannot abscond this impermanence!" roared Sir John, who gestured to the guards.

"Abide. Impertinence. Fruit." Ada's voice was clipped, but she never took her eyes off the fireplace.

Drina stepped forward and addressed the frustrated baronet. "Sir John, it does seem that we have some sort of pressing urgency at hand. Your assistance is greatly appreciated, and I shall most certainly be mindful to convey such appreciation to my dear mother upon her return."

Mary was terribly impressed by all of that, and couldn't imagine being able to deliver such a diplomatic speech in the middle of the night, at the age of nine or otherwise.

The princess continued: "I'm certain that my mother would approve, Sir John, and I shall be particularly grateful for your consideration of my personal safety."

"Safety?" Sir John may not have been sleepy, but he was easily confused.

"Indeed," interjected Mary. "Lady Ada here, no doubt with your assistance, has cornered the creature that has plagued the palace since goodness knows when."

"Wednesday," added Ada. "Since Wednesday."

"Caricature?" said Sir John, not sure if he should be pleased that he was being given credit, or angry at not having a clue as to what, precisely, was going on.

"Creature," corrected Ada. "Primates, Hominidae, *Pongo, P. pygmaeus.*"

"Please do excuse me," said Mary quietly, who gave the tiniest curtsy of her life before leaving.

"Honestly," said Ada, exasperated, "is it absolutely impossible to get a piece of fruit? Winter pears? An apple? Anything."

Baroness Lehzen stepped forward. "Pardon me," she said, addressing the palace guards. "You are . . . ?"

"Burke," said the first guard. "And this is Wally."

"Burke, Wally," resumed the baroness, "would you be so kind as to fetch a maid, or procure any sort of fruit you may encounter?"

"Very good, miss," said Burke.

"Miss Baroness," Wally tried to correct. The two trotted off down the hall, and Drina's little dog, Dash, decided to follow them in hopes they might do something interesting.

"She can't be a Miss Baroness" they could all hear from down the hall as the pair argued.

"Well, she's not a Highness," said Wally. "I don't think."

"A Middleness, then" was the reply.

"You're going to get us sacked, you know," Wally said.

Shortly, Mary returned with a brief apology, followed by a footman with sliced apples, pears, and raisins on a silver tray.

Mary selected a slice of apple and placed it in Ada's waiting fingers.

Ada slowly, carefully extended her arm into the unlit fireplace, and up the chimney. A moment later, she withdrew her hand, and the apple was gone.

"Again," she said.

Mary handed Ada another slice of fruit, and once more Ada placed her arm in and up the chimney. Only, this time she slowly withdrew it practically as soon as she inserted it.

The room gasped as one, as an impossibly long, red, hairy arm descended from the sooty chamber, with impossibly long grey fingers, groping about

for the apple, which Ada offered. The hand took its prize and retreated.

"That's right," Ada coaxed. "Come on out. There's more. That's it."

The arm returned, attached to a squat, shaggy body covered in red fur. Atop the barrel-shaped torso was its head, with a grey disk of a face and small, bright eyes.

It was indeed the face Mary had seen in the secret passage, and what was once a horror now seemed both kind and afraid.

"Faith!" exclaimed the baroness.

"Zooks!" exclaimed Sir John.

"Never you mind about them," Ada told the creature. "Come on."

The animal took a step out of the fireplace, and grasped Ada's hand. It put one finger on its lips as if it was considering what to do.

"Orangutan," Ada said. "From the *Bonnie Marguerite,* out of Borneo, to London for the circus. Stuck in the walls for days, poor thing."

"Oozmansvo denenvuk!" squawked Lory.

Smiling, the orangutan answered. The sounds were remarkably similar.

"Precisely," said Ada.

"Not Hungarian, or Croatian. Orangutan," Baroness Lehzen said in amazement.

"Cor, look at that 'andsome fellow," said Burke from the doorway, Wally behind nodding agreement.

The orangutan turned, and continued grinning. Drina took a slice of apple from the tray, and offered it to the grateful ape, who took it gently.

"But why did he go up the chimney?" asked Mary.

"Well, just now I think he went up there because he was frightened," said Ada. "And because he'd hidden there before. When the book went missing."

"What book?" demanded Sir John.

"One of the princess's sketchbooks, Sir John," explained Baroness Lehzen.

"You've told me nothing of a missing fishhook," he said huffily. "I am to be inflamed of everything!"

"Informed," corrected Ada.

Drina intervened. "I just noticed it was missing today, Sir John. I'm sure the baroness had no time to tell you until this moment."

"Well?" Sir John asked. "Where is it?"

"Orangutans," Ada began, "are gentle, curious creatures native to Borneo. This fellow was on a very long boat trip to England, and then was sent, or sold, to the circus. Clearly, he didn't think much of that, and escaped. He happened upon the palace, scaled the wall for safety, and discovered an unlocked window, in Drina's apartment."

Everyone nodded in unison, even the orangutan.

"Right, then here he is, terribly lost, when he enters this room, leaving a telltale bit of mud on the floor, and discovers the sketchbook in question. He has a brief conversation with Lory here—"

"Conversation!" squawked Lory.

"—and when startled, possibly by a maid who cleans up the mud, but not the trace of it under the door, our friend here finds the closest hiding place, up the chimney, leaving a stray red hair on his way up. He waits for the coast to clear. Then he sees someone"—and Ada here did her best not to emphasize the someone—"enter the secret passage, and follows. I fear he was trapped in there, until his recent release."

"That explains everything, Ada," said Mary, delighted. "Except the location of the sketchbook."

"Ah," Ada said. "I expect"—and she put her arm up the sooty chimney and felt about for a moment—"here. There's a little ledge . . ."

She held in her hand the book, bound in red linen but now quite grimy from the fireplace. She placed the filthy thing in Drina's grateful hands.

"Sorry," she added.

"Let me see that!" insisted Sir John. Rudely, he snatched the book from the young princess. Certain it was something secretive or incriminating, he examined it with a scowl. After a few pages, however, he relented.

"Dolls," he sighed, handing back the book with contempt.

"Indeed, Sir John," Drina said, "hardly noteworthy at all."

"Anyway, I think I felt something else up there," Ada said, straining once more up the chimney, blackening her sleeve in the process. "Got it."

In Ada's now coal-black hand shone an equally black object, a small figurine of a cat. Not exactly a cat, she discovered upon examination, but a cat with the head of a woman.

"Missing this?" Ada offered.

"Why, yes," said Drina. "I hadn't noticed, but it does go on the mantel."

The orangutan reached out to touch the cat figure as though it were a beloved pet.

"May I ask," asked Ada pointedly, "where this came from?"

"It was a gift," answered the baroness. "From your cousin. Medora Leigh."

"Why do you keep calling her that? Medora Leigh, I mean."

"Lady Ada," the baroness explained, "it is customary to use one's formal name at court. Even for your cousin Libby."

"One name in here," Ada said aloud to herself. "And another out there." She turned the object over in her hand. "A sphinx," she noted. "Of black quartz."

That phrase had turned up in the Wollstonecraft detectives' last case. The implications were . . . not good.

A GLIDER HOME

Mary awoke in Kensington Palace, in one of the many guest rooms. The early-morning light was made brighter by the cozy blanket of snow outside the leaded windows. Her previous night's adventure had let her sleep through the maid's careful laying of the fire, and she took in the moment to appreciate the luxury of it all. The quiet morning, the warm fire, the fine bedding. She may never again, she thought, awaken like a princess, so best to note every single detail, should she require it for a story.

But the story fragment that clung to her was not

one of royal grandeur, but one born of the terror from last night, gripping the rope, seeing the long stretches of winter earth as hard, and bitter, and desolate. Words came to her, and the room was of course furnished with a writing desk, paper, quill, and ink.

So immersed was Mary in her story that she did not hear the knock of the maid, inviting her to breakfast, and it took several discreet "ahems" to rouse her.

An hour later, washed and dressed and breakfasted with still no sign of either Drina or Ada, Mary found herself in the lush, exquisite hall.

Drina descended the stairs, her hand held tightly by the Baroness Lehzen. Both smiled broadly at Mary, who did her best curtsy. She was certain all of the Marylebone house would fit neatly between the grand front door and the staircase.

"Mary," said the princess. "How ever can I thank you? You have done me a tremendous kindness, you and Lady Ada both."

"Actually," said Mary, "I do have just a few questions."

"Certainly," said the baroness, in a tone that suggested they were free from being overheard.

"Where is Lady Ada?"

"She mentioned she had a conveyance of her own devising secured to the roof, and said she preferred to go home in that," Drina said, impressed. "And she has left you a note." Drina handed the folded, sealed parchment to Mary, who accepted it with a nod, bow, and curtsy all at once.

"How does it work?" Mary asked. "Your sketchbook, I mean."

Drina reflexively glanced left and right, leaning slightly closer.

"Each doll is a different day. A hat represents one feeling, a dress another. The colors matter, too, and even though I just draw them with pen and ink, I know what the color of each thing is. It's nothing so dramatic, just my own thoughts and feelings, but private all the same. The only thing I have that is. That's why it mattered so."

"A code," said Mary.

"A code," said Drina.

"Thank you," Mary said. Asking further on the subject would be prying, so she changed tack. "And our ape friend?"

"He is in the care of Burke and Wally. They are extraordinarily fond of him, and have sworn to see him returned to his home."

"To Borneo?" Mary marveled.

"It appears they wish to accompany him, so I have released them from service, by their request," said Drina.

"One more question. Eagle mid rho? That was you?" Mary asked.

"It was," said Drina with a small smile.

"Good clue!" Mary acknowledged.

"It's not mine, I must confess. Lady Ada's cousin Medora Leigh discovered the passage upon one of her visits. She referred to it thusly, that I should remember it."

"Well, it's awfully clever," said Mary.

And then everything made a horrible, horrible kind of sense.

Mary felt herself turning grey. Everything she

had learned from the first moment she had become friends with Ada jumped up and down, clamoring in her brain for attention.

Eagle mid rho.

Image held, or.

Medora Leigh.

Anagrams. Word scrambles, all different, but the same letters. A secret code for secret passages.

The girl who pretended friendship to the princess was the same girl who lurked behind the mirror, writing a boast about how foolish the princess was to trust her. It struck Mary as being so tremendously clever and impossibly wicked at the same time.

"I say, Miss Mary, are you quite well?" the baroness asked.

But Mary was not well. As the Ada-bits of Mary's brain grew louder, so did Mary's heart feel as if it were retreating in her chest, running away from the awfulness the clues presented her.

"Drina," Mary said quietly. "I know you're made to feel self-conscious about your accent, and I assure you, you do not have one. Not the slightest. But still, you speak German, yes?"

"Yes," said Drina, if a little shyly.

"Eagle mid rho. What is the German word for 'eagle'?" Mary thought she knew, had heard it or read it somewhere, and wished fervently that she had not, wished she were wrong.

"Adler," stated Drina plainly.

Mary, it turned out, had not been wrong.

Eagle mid rho was Medora Leigh, and "eagle" also meant *"Adler."*

And *"Adler"* was Radel.

Nora Radel, Ada's nemesis. A criminal mastermind, and lover of word games, the supposedly cleverest girl in England, whose code name was the Sphinx of Black Quartz. Like the black-quartz sphinx given to a princess by a girl named Medora Leigh, who was also called Libby, who was Ada's own cousin.

Mary practically fainted on the spot, but her courage prevailed and she gathered her senses.

"Please do promise me," Mary managed to get

out, "that under no circumstances will you entertain Ada's cousin until you hear from us. I fear . . ." But Mary couldn't find the words for what she feared. And so she settled for "Please. She is not . . . as she seems."

Drina and the baroness said nothing, merely looking at one another, and nodding in seriousness.

Farewells were said. Mary for the last time stepped into the enchantment of the magnificent carriage and noticed almost none of it, so desperate was she to consult with Ada. Her heart was banging about her chest—she could scarcely believe what she had realized. She tried to calm herself, go over the variables just as Ada would, but it was to no avail. Her imagination spun possible plots and machinations faster than her reason could sort them.

There was, however, one brief instant when she could swear she snatched a glimpse of bat wings, soaring over London.

It was at that moment she realized she held in her hand the note that Ada had given Drina, and that Drina had given her.

Anxiously, she popped the wax of the seal. She

unfolded the note, on palace stationery, to reveal a single, brief sentence written in the hand of a twelve-year-old genius.

The note simply stated:

"I know."

ENOUGH

All was abuzz at the Godwin house for dinner on Christmas Eve. Mary and Jane laughed and worked in the kitchen like wooden figures in a cuckoo clock, spinning and stepping and never crashing into one another. Their older sister, Fanny, labored tirelessly alongside Mrs. Godwin, who sang merry little songs in French, and they all glowed as much from happiness as from the heat in the small room. The scent of goose, of cinnamon and nutmeg and plum sauce, enlivened the air, and in the next room, Mr. Godwin was managing both the baby and the stringing of garlands by the fire. All was cozy and festive, warm and welcoming.

Guests arrived with cheer: first Mr. and Mrs. Woolcott with their ward, Allegra, who gave a knowing wink to Mary and could not wait to explain how simple it was to escape from iron shackles with a snick knife and a modicum of savvy. The Woolcotts were warmed with mulled cider spiced with cloves, and the dusting of snow that had settled upon shawls and hats first melted and then steamed away in the homey, book-strewn apartment.

Next to arrive was Peebs, fresh from his journey, bearing letters for Mr. Godwin and novels for the girls, who accepted their gifts with broad smiles.

"La, Peebs, we've been having such an adventure!" Mary said, handing him a warm cup.

"I'm glad you're well, Mary," Peebs said. "I do look forward to hearing all about it."

"Have you seen Ada?"

"No," Peebs replied. "I've only just arrived in London. It so happened that I came across some papers I thought might be of some interest to your father, and popped 'round to wish you all a happy Christmas."

Mary was about to regale her tutor with her tale of a spied-upon princess, a secret book, a hidden passage, and an exotic orangutan but was cut short by a knock on the door. Seeing that everyone had their hands full in preparation for dinner, and that Allegra was attempting to do a handstand in the crowded parlor despite Mrs. Woolcott's protestations, Mary excused herself to answer the door.

"Charles!" Mary exclaimed, delighted. "Happy Christmas!"

"And to you, Mary," said Mary's friend with a grin. "I've just arrived home and wanted to wish the very best to you and yours."

"Oh, do come in," Mary pleaded.

But Charles couldn't stay long. After a hearty thank-you to Peebs for recommending him for his new position, he cheerfully made his way to his own family's new home.

Mary returned to the kitchen then, where Mrs. Godwin was bringing out the goose, to a great deal of oohing and aahing. There was another knock, only this one barely audible. Not because it was a soft knock but because of the din of the party—and this knock was farther away.

Mary handed off a bundle of spoons to Jane, and trotted down the stairs to the door of the Polygon building itself. She opened the door, and a gust of snow blew in.

The carriage waiting outside resembled a black cake dusted in sugar. And between the carriage and the door stood Ada.

"Ada!"

Mary embraced her, and Ada's shoulders rose into her ears as her only response to the hug.

"Oh, yes, I'm sorry," Mary apologized, remembering that Ada was not always fond of being squished so. "Please, do come in."

"No," said Ada cheerfully. "It's all a bit people-y in there, I expect, but I am glad to see you."

"There's so much, I don't know where to begin! Your cousin Libby—"

"Is Nora Radel. And a criminal mastermind. I know. And you know—well done, Mary. Nobody else knows, though. Well, she knows, of course. But

I don't think she knows we know. Yet. Anyway. I need a plan."

"You'll come up with one, I'm sure of it."

"I should hope so," said Ada. "I've just come from the docks. The *Bonnie Marguerite* set sail this afternoon, with the orangutan. And those two guards, gone with him."

"Well, it was good of you to see them off."

"Mmm," said Ada. "I have a thing."

"A thing?" Mary asked.

"Here," said Ada, and handed Mary a large, hastily folded square of brown paper. Mary unfolded it, and there in the light of the street, she saw a drawing, or many sketches and notes for what looked like a statue, or a mechanical horse, with wings like the mythical Pegasus. It was intricate, and fantastical, and marvelous.

"It's part of my flyology project. Anyway, I thought you'd . . . understand it."

"I do, Ada, at least I think I do. Are you going to build it?"

"It would be useful, at least until I get my balloon back, once I sort out how, exactly."

"Don't you need these plans?"

"Oh, I'll remember them," said Ada confidently. "Anyway, I just . . . I wanted . . ."

"Thank you, Ada. It's a lovely Christmas present." Mary folded it up again, as the paper was becoming dappled by the snow.

Ada just nodded, and stepped back toward the waiting carriage.

171

"Happy Christmas, Ada!" shouted Mary as the carriage pulled away.

All Mary could see were Ada's gloved fingers, pressed against the glass. But she understood all Ada meant with that gesture. And that was enough.

NOTES

THE REGENCY

The period between the end of the 1700s and the year Queen Victoria took the British throne is generally referred to as the Regency. If the Victorian era was a game that changed the shape of the world, the Regency was when all the pieces were placed on the board.

In 1826, the future queen Victoria (Princess Drina) was only seven years old. The world had seen a recent flurry of inventions: Volta's electric battery (1800), Fulton's submarine and torpedo (1800), Winsor's patented gas lighting (1804), Trevithick's steam locomotive (1804), Davy's electric arc light (1809), Bell's steam-powered boat (1812), and Sturgeon's electromagnet (1824). It was an exciting time of technological advancement, and it brought forth two very bright girls who changed the world through their intellect and imagination.

The lives of women—and particularly girls—were extremely limited and under constant watch. Women were not allowed to vote or practice professions, and were widely thought to be less capable than men. A girl's value to her family was in her reputation and her service, and she was expected to obediently accept a husband of her parents' choosing. Any threat to that reputation—like behaving unusually—was often enough to ruin a family.

However, because girls were not expected to have a career and compete with their (or anybody's) husband, upper-class girls were free to read or study as they wished, for few took them seriously. Because of this rare freedom, the nineteenth century saw a sharp surge in the intellectual contributions of female scientists and mathematicians, with Ada foremost among them.

AUGUSTA ADA BYRON (1815–1852) was a brilliant mathematician and the daughter of the poet Lord

ADA

Byron (who died when Ada was eight). Largely abandoned by her mother, she was raised by servants (and sometimes her grandmother) at the Marylebone house and was very much cut off from the world as a child.

With her legendary temper and lack of social skills (a modern historian unkindly calls her "mad as a hatter"), Ada made few friends. Her mother insisted that young Ada have no connection to her father's friends or even his interests, so Ada turned to mathematics. As a teenager, she worked with her friend Charles Babbage on the tables of numbers for Babbage's "Analytical Engine"—a mechanical computer—which was not built in his lifetime. But Ada's contribution to the work, as well as her idea that computers could be used not only for mathematics but also for creative works such as music, has caused many people to refer to Ada as "the world's first computer programmer." Babbage called her the Enchantress of Numbers. Her inventiveness was not limited to mathematics. Just as described in this book, she really did invent "flyology" as a field of study, wrote a book by that name, and drew the blueprints for a steam-powered flying horse.

Ada was married at nineteen to William King, a baron, who became the Count of Lovelace three years later. This is why Ada is more commonly known as Ada Lovelace. She had three children—Byron, Annabella, and Ralph—and died of cancer at the age of thirty-six. She continues to inspire scientists and mathematicians to this day, and many worthwhile projects are named after her.

MARY WOLLSTONECRAFT GODWIN (1797–1851) was the daughter of the famous feminist writer Mary Wollstonecraft (who died ten days after giving birth) and the political philosopher William Godwin. William Godwin married the publisher Mary Jane Clairmont in 1801, and Mary grew up in a mixed household of half siblings and stepsiblings in Somers Town, in northern London. She read broadly and had an appetite for adventure and romanticism. She ran away with Percy Shelley at age sixteen, and over one very famous weekend with Shelley, Lord Byron (Ada's father), and early vampire novelist Dr. John Polidori, Mary came up with the idea for the world's first science-fiction novel—*Frankenstein; or, The Modern Prometheus*—which she wrote at age nineteen.

In real life, Mary was eighteen years older than Ada. But I thought it would be more fun this way—to cast these two luminaries as friends.

CLARA ALLEGRA (ALBA) BYRON (1817–1822) was the daughter of Claire Clairmont and Lord Byron. Her mother could not care for her, so she was left with her father. He, however, frequently left her in the care of strangers, eventually placing her in a convent in Italy. She died of fever at the age of five, but I have moved her timeline and brought her to life in the world of Wollstonecraft, to be a truer sister to Ada.

PEEBS

PERCY BYSSHE (rhymes with "fish") SHELLEY (1792–1822) was an important poet and best friend to Ada's father, Lord Byron. Percy came from a wealthy family, and he offered to support Mary's father and the Godwin family. At age twenty-two, he ran off with then-sixteen-year-old Mary to Switzerland, and they were married two years later. He drowned at the age of twenty-nine when his sailboat sank in a storm.

While in reality, Peebs had died even before our story begins, I have extended his life so that they can be in this story together. It is Peebs, as Ada's father's friend and Mary's future husband, who provides a real-life link between our two heroines.

CHARLES DICKENS (1812–1870) is considered one of the great writers of Victorian England. He really did work for the law firm of Ellis and Blackmore—though not because of a referral from Peebs! He loved books and was a keen observer of everyday life in London. He is perhaps best known to young readers as the author of *A Christmas Carol*.

CLARA ("CLAIRE") MARY JANE CLAIRMONT (1798–1879) was known as Jane as a child but later adopted the name Claire. She really was Mary's stepsister (her mother married Mary's father), but her real life diverges dramatically from this story. Jane was actually Allegra's mother! I adjusted her timeline and role so that the two sets of sisters—Ada and Allegra, Mary and Jane—could work together as friends and detectives.

DRINA

PRINCESS ALEXANDRINA VICTORIA (QUEEN VICTORIA) (1819–1901) was queen of the United Kingdom of Great Britain and Ireland and empress of India. As queen, she saw the map of the world change under her leadership and inspiration, giving shape to the modern era both politically and economically.

As a young girl and "heir presumptive," she was raised apart from other children in a very controlled and lonely way, with her every mood or activity closely watched. Little details, such as her dolls, her drawings, her parrot, her dog, and even her insecurities, are all drawn from real life, though I have aged her a tiny bit for this story.

She was constantly manipulated by her mother, the Princess Victoria, and her mother's adviser Lord Conroy, in hopes of securing a strong position for them both once Drina became queen. But their plan backfired—Drina only let Conroy remain in the palace on the condition that she never saw him or knew he was there.

JOHANNA CLARA LOUISE LEHZEN (1784–1870) was the German-born governess to Princess Drina and one of her few allies in the palace. While Drina's mother and her adviser tried to keep Drina weak and ill-informed, Baroness Lehzen worked to shape the young princess into a strong and capable woman.

SIR JOHN PONSONBY CONROY (1786–1854) was an ambitious army officer who tried to control the young Drina's household through manipulation and surveillance. He was unceasingly cruel to the princess and was nearly banished when she became queen.

This is a short story by Edgar Allan Poe written in 1841 and often considered the first detective story in English. I have borrowed its solution here for the book's end—an orangutan up the chimney!

The Polygon was a fifteen-sided apartment building in Clarendon Square in Somers Town, in what was then the northern part of London (the city has long since grown around it). It was home to the Godwin family and, later, to Charles Dickens. Dickens wrote about the Polygon, making it the home of Harold Skimpole in the novel *Bleak*

House. Scholars have speculated that the character of Skimpole may have been based on Mary's father, William Godwin. While the building is long gone, the road that bears its name remains.